FIGHTING FATE

DIANA MUÑOZ STEWART

Fighting Fate, copyright 2023, Diana Muñoz Stewart
Published by Diana Muñoz Stewart
Cover by Elizabeth Mackey
Layout by www.formatting4U.com

Dedicated to my mother.
For her laughter, love, and guidance.

Other Books by Diana Muñoz Stewart

HIDDEN JUSTICE (Spy Makers Guild Book 1)
RECKLESS GRACE (Spy Makers Guild Book 2)
DARING HONOR (Spy Makers Guild Book 3)

*BROKEN PROMISES (*Bad Legacy Book 1*)*
*AMOR ACTUALLY (*A holiday anthology)

UPCOMING RELEASES by Diana Muñoz Stewart

IT'S ALL IN THE HIPS (Stand-alone, Coming December 2023)
TO-BE-NAMED ANTHOLOGY (February 2024)
SOFT PROMISES (Bad Legacy Book 2, Coming July 2024)

Prologue

Sean

Feeling like Gulliver in the land of Lilliputians, I labor around the hut, commenting on and admiring the artwork of the Salvadoran children whom I've asked to draw what home feels like. Their paintings are as sweet as they are shocking, with a mixture of hope, love, grief, and unflinching violence.

Despite the harsh realities and sometimes treacherous gang factions in El Salvador, there's nowhere I'd rather be—a bit of a shock for this Welshman.

Six years ago, drunk and unhappy, I would've sworn nothing in life could ever bring me joy again. Not after losing my one and only love—football.

Looking back now, I barely feel I know that sulky bastard, the almost-famous Sean Bradford. That lucky sod played the beautiful game with an aggressive ease that earned fans, women, money, and nearly the contract that would've set him up for life.

But for the accident.

If it could be called an accident. My throat fills with heat, but the once-choking bitterness barely burns now. Volunteering for Artist Without Borders gave me a much-needed reality check and helped transform the turmoil in my mind.

Hard to believe I nearly let the drink take me, but life gave me a second chance. One I try to extend to these kids every day.

Stopping by the easel of a young artist, a gang kid, maybe ten—boys here are recruited early—I offer him the praise he deserves and needs. "Excellente, Pedro. Muy bonito."

Clutching his paintbrush awkwardly in a hand mangled by a violence I can only guess at, he shrugs and rolls his eyes. The tough guy. These children crave approval as much as they fear *showing* they crave it. Bloody shame.

That need, as much as the art, is why I'm here. Probably seems daft to some. What can art bring to children caught in a land so violent that a huge percentage joins gangs to protect themselves from gangs? People who'd walk thousands of kilometers to reach El Norte—the North.

But what those critics don't understand is what I know from experience: art can rescue the soul.

Stopping by another easel, I admire the girl's raw talent. At thirteen, Sofía has an ability that would make the gods weep. To think that such a gift as hers could've been lost to the careless chance of her birthplace… Breaks the heart. Not only her talent, but the life of her, the sheer joy of a spirit her father works so very hard to keep safe from the gangs that would take this bud on the cusp of womanhood. The lads here aren't the only ones the gangs take. Her father, a good man, is outside right now, waiting to get his little artist home safely.

Unlike Pedro, Sofía smiles up at me with reddish-brown eyes as innocent and trusting as the streaks of pink across her canvas.

"That's lovely," I tell her, using English because she's trying to learn the language.

She angles her head, looking back at her canvas. "Señor Sean, does the sky look the same in Wales?"

"Aye, it does. And you've captured it perfectly."

All sharp cheeks and teen awkwardness, she grins. "It's for you. A gift, so you'll remember your promise to come back."

Remorse tightens my shoulder blades. I wish I could stay longer, but the funding has run out. When I joined AWB three years ago, I'd used my celebrity—what there was of it—to secure funding to launch into Central America. But out of sight, out of mind. Funds have dried up, so now I need to head home and make some appearances to raise more money. “I will take this lovely painting, but I insist on paying your first commission as an artist.”

Brown cheeks blooming with red, she shakes head. “No. You can give that money to AWB, so you can come back. I have more to learn.” She points to the others in the room. “We all do.”

The heat is back in my throat, along with a knot. “I’m coming back, Sofía. Promise.”

Gunshots from outside send my nerves jumping and the students diving from the crates that serve as stools.

I grab Sofía, drag her to the ground, then cover her body with my own. Shouts and screams flow through the window and everything escalates in one life-shattering instant.

Sofía’s father runs into the room, bleeding from a wound in his chest.

Two men holding guns follow him.

I know without being told why they’re here or, more likely, who they’re here to get. Sofía isn’t only a budding artist, but a budding beauty. That’s why her father brings her here to keep her safe. It’s why he’s bleeding out on the floor.

And it’s why I get to my feet and face the men with guns and the three other men who come in behind them.

They will take her over my dead body.

Chapter 1
Dada

I've been undercover as a nun for approximately two hours and have already lost my ability to lie convincingly. A problem, considering lying is a basic job requirement for spies, especially those not authorized by any government.

Standing inside the convent's brick-lined, plant-heavy courtyard, I try to take back my statement. "Perdoname, Sister Angelica, I… I…" Stupendous—how do a black habit and a white tunic suddenly make me Maria from *The Sound of Music*? "I didn't mean to suggest these habits aren't the highest of fashion—"

The *highest of fashion*? Aren't they designed to be the exact *opposite* of fashion? What's happening to me?

Could this be the disguise that ruins ten years of doing covert operations for The Guild?

Impossible. I've taken on dozens of false identities: wealthy Nigerian heiress, international model, security guard, translator, Special Envoy to the UN, to name a few. Leaving behind my real identity as Dada Parish and assuming a new one is as easy as putting on a coat—or *had* been before I came to Mexico and gazed into Sister Angelica's serious blue eyes, framed by those demanding black-rimmed glasses.

Honestly, this woman could be my polar opposite. She's short—under five feet—with silver curls peeking from beneath her habit, and skin as white as talcum powder. The only thing about us that matches is our outfits.

And maybe our temperaments.

Palm resting on her cane, Sister Angelica fans her fingers. "No apology necessary. If I took affront at every little thing, Sister Dee, I'd be a piss-poor servant of God. Besides, I agree; these habits *do* belong in a musical."

Piss-poor? Definitely *not* a nun thing to bark laughter when being introduced to my new abbess.

Holding on to my trademark calm, I smile. "Gracias, Sister Angelica."

The abbess shakes off the thanks. "Stop the men trafficking women through Mexico. That, more than the money your mother donated, will be thanks enough."

Keeping my face placid despite the fact that this woman spoke the truth about my reconnaissance mission aloud *and* the fact that my mother—wealthy founder and head of the Spy Makers Guild—is funding it, should earn me top honors.

I maintain eye contact with her and the slight flush of her lined cheeks is the sign I'm looking for that she understands her mistake, and not a moment too soon as raised voices funnel through the corridor.

A bevy of nuns, as diverse as my adopted family, flows into the courtyard and surrounds us, greeting me with a mixture of curiosity, eagerness, and various Spanish accents.

"Hermana Dee, estás aquí."

"Not a moment too soon."

"Serendipity."

"You should come with us."

"Yes, come," the final nun says with the directness of someone who has lived beyond forty.

I blink at her round, reddish-tan face and gap-toothed smile.

"I'm Lupe." Grabbing me by the arm, Lupe spins me toward the door and says, "If we don't hurry, we won't be ready for the lunch crowd."

"Lunch crowd?" I say as the morning sun heats my face and I realize I've been unceremoniously dragged back onto the streets of Oaxaca with its tightly lined, colorful buildings.

Sister Angelica closes the door with a gentle, “I’ll see your bag gets to your room.”

Stupendous. Nuns, it turns out, are a little bossy.

* * *

Ten minutes after walking into the Benedictine abbey that serves as my cover, I find myself standing behind the counter of a soup kitchen, doling out arroz con pollo y frijoles to a line of hungry people. Ah, the glamorous life of a spy.

Clouds of heat waft up from the steel food well and moisture slides from under my habit and along my face. Even with my shorn hair, I’m sweating.

Despite my discomfort, I offer ready smiles and warm greetings to the numerous refugees filing along the open-air cafeteria. As well I should, because these people have it a lot worse than me.

Thanks to my heritage, I have few problems communicating with the mostly Spanish speakers making their way north from Central and South America. I can even change my Puerto Rican accent to mirror that of Mexico. The five languages I speak are part of what makes me a good undercover agent.

If only being a nun came as easily. Let’s be honest, I suck at it. And it’s not like I haven’t done my research because I definitely have. No, it’s the social cues. For example, no nun reacts to music, but I have to physically stop myself from swaying my hips to the worn guitar a man plays at one of the tables.

I sigh out loud as the music stops then, nearly as one, the sisters pause serving the food, and one after another, their heads swing left.

I look around for what caused the response. Actually, not *what*.

Who.

Six-feet-something, and that something is fine with a capital F. Wavy auburn hair, sexy trimmed beard, and summer-brown eyes. The kind of toned body that a man can't hide, even under the long-sleeved over-shirt that suggests conceal-carry. Sean Bradford. The man I'm here to meet. Not that he knows that.

Unbidden, the memory of him as a sleek young man driving down the soccer pitch surfaces, along with a surge of admiration and longing. I remember watching him with my heart in my throat and my eyes glued to the screen.

He'd been an amazing player, beautiful and sure-footed, but he'd been injured right before signing a contract in the Premier League. Most people probably wouldn't remember him or recognize this version of him, bearded and older.

I'm not most people.

I've been known to get up at all hours to watch games from overseas. It's the one thing I remember of my papi. Long ago, we'd watch matches together in Puerto Rico.

When I saw Sean's face on recon photos my family took of the traffickers, I'd recognized him. A deep dive, including my brother Tony flying down to El Salvador, gave us the whole story. And a way to use Sean as an asset.

Despite Sean's limp, he walks with a confident swagger. Yum, he is glorious—a very un-nun-like thought to have. Except, it's not only me reacting to him. Why did everyone go so still when he appeared? Do people here know his history?

I brush Lupe's shoulder and pretend ignorance. "Who is he?"

Lupe's bright expression sours. "Juan the Forger. Works for traffickers—men aligned with the cartel that own this area. He donates every week"—she nods toward the donation boxes dotting the room—"then takes a tray for an older woman in town who can't leave her home."

"You don't approve of him doing kind things?"

Scooping yellow rice for the next-in-line, Lupe shakes her head. "He does bad, *allows* bad, because he benefits from it then, to assuage his guilt, he donates. I do not approve."

With her words comes genuine pain for this man, because I *know* his story. Eighteen months ago, Sean went up against men trying to take an art student from his studio in El Salvador. When he resisted, they nearly beat him to death.

Three months later, he was finally able to leave the hospital. That very day, he packed a bag and walked out of El Salvador, joining a caravan of refugees going north.

Now, he's in an impossible situation, trying desperately to stay on the fringes of what the slavers are doing, but also trying to find the child he fought to keep from being taken.

I can help him… assuming he helps me.

My heart ratchets up as Sean swaggers closer. Each of my heartbeats, like a cart ascending on a roller coaster, clicks higher and higher into my throat.

Oh, no. Nope. I *can't* develop feelings for him.

Squaring my shoulders, I slap down my attraction and put it in chains. Chains as heavy as my determination. How ironic that, after a lifetime of denying my wants and needs, the one disguise that requires I do just that has my libido rebelling like a teenager.

After accepting a scoop of rice, Sean stops in front of me for frijoles. My fool heart, obviously not having gotten the no-lust memo, jumps as Sean's eyes widen then take me in. His hungry gaze skims down my body. It does not help that my fool body reacts, heat cascading through me. Not needed. I'm already sweating.

I'm so unwillingly turned on by those gorgeous brown eyes framed in a bounty of lashes that I forget for a moment where I'm at, what I'm supposed to be doing, and who I'm supposed to be. Ay. Dios.

Beside me, Sister Lupe says, "Do you want beans or are you filling your belly looking at Sister Dee?"

His pale skin flushes. "Disculpe, Hermana. Frijoles, por favor."

His Spanish is good as he apologizes and asks for beans, but I can definitely hear his Welsh accent.

Heart still in my throat, I scoop the beans into a small paper cup, then hand them to him.

Our fingers brush. A strong, certain flash of awareness shoots up my arm and down my spine. A visceral response. A longing. A knowing. A wanting.

A big complication.

The attraction between us is thick and impossible to deny. It's the reason I'm not pulling my hand back. The reason he hasn't either. The reason our gazes have collided and held.

Beside me, Sister Lupe clears her throat.

Sean's face reddens even more. He springs back, nearly spilling his beans. He moves off with a gruffly mumbled, "Sorry, Sister. Sorry."

No need to ask what he's apologizing for. It's obvious. One does not make lust-eyes at a nun.

Chapter 2

Sean

Face as hot as my assured eternal damnation, I practically run from the soup kitchen, making my way around the locals and refugees crowding the sidewalk. Did I just make eyes at a nun? Merciful heaven, I need to have sex. Been too long.

Likely, I'm destined for Hell. The Devil is probably preparing my bed right now. *Here, boyo, lie down on this dry straw.* Right smack dab in the middle of hellfire.

Not that any man wouldn't have noticed her. She was so vibrant, so sexy, so… Good Lord, I'm doing it again! *Stop it, daft bugger. There's a line of thinking you need to step away from, drive away from, speed like hell fire away from.*

Just hadn't expected… skin as silky as the finest sheets. And her eyes, so direct, like she knew me. Like she wanted me. Like… she knew my soul is destined for Hell. Ach!

"Hold on, there. Hold on, please."

The whisky voice slides into my stomach and warms it. That's a good voice.

I turn. Bollocks. It's her, jogging down the sidewalk, her breasts bouncing under her—

Nun tunic, *you perv.*

She slows, then points at my hands. "I'm sorry. You can't take the tray."

What? I glance down with dawning horror. *Ach y fi.* I'd been so determined to get out of there I'd forgotten. "Sorry, Sister…

"Desdemona. Dee for short."

"Juan, Sister Dee," I mumble, though I feel foolish lying to her about my name, as she's spoken to me in English and can surely see I'm not from around here. I attempt to balance the tray and slip off my backpack.

"Just Dee," she says, reaching forward. She licks her lips with a pink tongue. The pinkest tongue I've ever seen. "Let me hold it for you."

Hold *what*?

Christ, man—the *tray*. She means *the tray*.

Hellfire. Think about that.

"Thanks, Sister." I hand her the tray and take off my backpack. I'm fishing out containers when I spot Armand across the street, smoking a joint. I grind my teeth. This is Walid's man. We've clashed many times since I've started making papers for Walid.

I can't stand the bloke. Even at this distance, he exudes menace. The man has had it out for me for a long time, but the look he's giving me now is pure hatred.

Not sure what I've done this time. In the past, he's been bothered by the money I give to the poor, by the fact that I take food to my neighbor, by the fact that I refuse to do certain papers for his boss. If I weren't so good at my job making global passports and visas, I'm sure he'd make me disappear.

He might just, judging by the look he's giving me. I shrug it off because I've given up a lot of my morality in my search for Sofía and in my attempt to make up for the foolish chance I took starting an art class in an area that required an excess of caution, but I'm not going to give up on common decency.

I transfer the food from the tray. When done, Sister Dee smiles at me.

"I saw you play. Before your injury, I mean."

Fuck. Balls. Fuck. I dare not glance back at Armand, not that he can hear from here, but it's still not safe. "Not sure what you're talking about."

Her smile widens, as if unbothered by my lie. Probably used to degenerates lying to her.

She says, "Juan is a form of John. And Sean is the Welsh form of John. Your name when you played, soccer… ah, you call it football… was Sean Bradford. Clever."

Not so clever. She'd picked that apart in two seconds. Tidy. And a sports fan. And hot as hell. *And a nun.* Shame. "I'm not interested in being that guy, Sister."

"Dee."

"Sister Dee."

"Just Dee."

Why does she have to be kind and lovely? "I'm not interested in being that guy, Dee." I lower my voice, trying to emphasize the real point. "I *can't* be that guy. Not here. Might seal my fate, if you know what I mean."

Her eyes turn serious and maybe a little surprised. She fiddles with the tray. "Of course. Sorry. Pero don't fear Señora Fate."

"What?"

"She's not destiny at first, you know." She meets my eyes so directly that I nod as if agreeing, though there's no cause for it. "She's challenge. If you decline her challenge, Fate will write your story for you. If you accept her challenge, even if you don't succeed at first… Well, then, everything changes."

"That so?" I find myself smiling down at her.

"It is. I've learned to accept and jump at chances before I even recognize what benefit they might bring. In turn, I accept and muster through complications, knowing Fate will bend in my favor if I only persist."

"Ah, so you take Fate in your own hands." And because I'm an idiot, I add, "You're not what I expected."

A sly grin spreads across her beautiful face. "Not the first time I've heard that."

That, I don't doubt. We stare at each other, and every part of me feels enthralled by a woman as kind and positive as she is beautiful.

"Thanks for your help, luv—uh, Sister. I mean, Dee."

Feeling like an absolute sod, I flee before I can get myself into any more trouble. I give one more bit of attention to Armand, hoping to nod in his direction or do something to let him know I won't be intimidated by his glare.

But he isn't looking at me. My fists clench when I notice who he *is* watching. His glare, the daggers and ice look in his eyes, is riveted on Sister Dee.

Chapter 3

Armand

Through the swirling smoke rising from the joint pinched between my nails, I watch the nun and Juan the Forger.

Acrid relief glides down my throat, then nestles into my lungs as I bite back breath. Ash floats from the joint to land on then disappear against my skin, and I blow off the white flakes with my exhale.

Even drugs can't dilute this rage. Why is this woman dressed as a nun? My gut rejects the notion that she's actually a woman of God. Not that it matters to me if she really is, because luck has delivered her to me, and I don't ignore opportunity.

A man passing by on the street stops and blocks my view. "You can't smoke here," he says, pointing to the bar's No Smoking sign shaded by the faded awning.

American, judging by his accent and his ugly shoes. Also, if he'd been from around here, he wouldn't have said a word. Not just because I'm imposing and scarred, but because all here know me.

Giving the pendejo a look that would curl the blood of any beast with sense, a look that gooses the man and sends him shuffling off, I take another deep drag.

Across the street, the whore nun walks away with a tray tucked under her arm.

She doesn't look my way, but, even if she had, she wouldn't pay me any attention. Not like I pay her attention, but then again, unlike me, she is beautiful.

A beauty that makes me ill. It's as Mother often said, "If

there is character, ugliness becomes beauty. If there is none, beauty becomes ugliness."

I know how to make sure the outside of this woman matches the inside. A desire to do so rises into my smoke-sore throat. My phone buzzes, and I take out my cell. Glancing at the number on the screen I wince. Walid.

There's no way not to answer him. Grinding out the blunt with my fingers, I say, "Here."

"Where is here?" Walid asks. "Not where you should be, which is at my front gate doing your job. Do you have somewhere else you need to be?"

Red fury bursts through my body with such heat I sweat it melts the filling in my grinding teeth. My mother—the earth surely rotten where she's been laid to rest—would challenge me in the same demeaning way. If not for the girls and protection Walid offers, I wouldn't put up with the way he talks to me.

I won't have to put up with it much longer.

"I was just headed back from town after seeing to"—I pause as if searching for a word and then fill my voice with repressed disgust—"your entertainers."

There's a longer pause on Walid's end, and I can tell the dig at him has hit its mark. Despite all Walid's wealth, he is weak, because he's a grown man who still thinks of himself as a little brother.

His raspy voice fills the line again, but with a lot less venom. "The last shipment sent to the Americas… you oversaw it, no?"

My moment of satisfaction slips away as a worm of dread twists in my gut. To be caught stealing from Walid—and, more importantly, his older brother Aamir—would earn me a brutal and sadistic death. "I did."

"My man in the States tells me an item is missing. Do you know what I mean?"

"A missing item?" In all the years I've been stealing girls from Walid, he's never challenged me about the women I've taken. And I remember this last one, a plump, doe-eyed girl… What's the big deal? "Yes. I'm handling it."

"So, you know where my merchandise is?"

I know exactly where she's buried, and how long she screamed, cried, and begged for mercy. "I've men out looking. Not to worry."

"I don't want reassurances. Reassurances are something for women and children when you direct them to the gas chamber. I want to know how this happened, where it happened, and who is looking for the item. Come with these answers. Now."

He hangs up.

I stare at my phone a moment, wishing I could reach through the line and end the man. Since that isn't possible, I call the only number I have memorized.

My partner answers after one ring. "Yes?"

"We need to replace that girl, the doe-eyed one. Start looking among the refugees."

"I'll see to it." The line is uttered with a tone as flat and determined as the man's personality. He's a good second-in-command. Together, we've established a growing side business dedicated to the discerning man who literally wants to screw a woman to death.

Soon, we'll have enough money to relocate, but not now. Now, is a dangerous time, a time I can ill afford to get caught taking from Walid. I'll have to shift my focus back to the town. If I don't take too many, no one really notices missing women. Of course, there is one exception to that rule.

"I'll also need your help in covering the disappearance of a nun."

There's a long moment of silence, and I know he's thinking about the fallout. The people here are very religious. Taking a refugee is one thing, and attracts little notice if not done too often, but taking a nun…

"A nun will be difficult."

"More difficult than saving your life?"

There is another pause on the line, and this one is longer and heavier. "We'll have to burn the body."

Chapter 4

Dada

A warm gust molds my tunic against my thighs as I stroll as quickly as possible down the cobbled streets of the town square. The other sisters won't like that I'm late for the lunch rush, which is becoming my habit—along with nun puns.

I've been a nun for a week. I still suck at it. Not only the shift in my persona, but the difficulty of trying to balance undercover operations and nun activities. Four AM prayers? Totally draining. If I were in a more lenient disguise, I could enjoy sunny Oaxaca, with its historic buildings, terra-cotta tiled roofs, stone arches, and steepled white churches. As it is, I can only gaze longingly as I pass carts of different wares and yummy food lining plaza de la ciudad.

Probably for the best. I'm here to do a job. Knowing this, my trained gaze sweeps the people eating at cozy tables, vendors chatting with customers, couples walking hand-and-hand, and a smiling toddler pulling a wheeled, wooden cockatoo. He's so cute in tiny jeans that cover his little marching legs.

The ache of loss thickens in my throat, and I absently run fingers along my worn leather bracelet. It's a reminder that I survived captivity, and that I need to prove worthy of the gift Momma gave me when she rescued and adopted me. I should've died giving birth alone. Part of my heart died, part of my soul, along with my infant son, but I survived.

I push aside the long-held pain. I'm an undercover operative in The Guild and here to rescue others, not to indulge in what-ifs.

Even so, my attention falls one last time on the boy, and I see him freeze in his tracks. Two men, twenty-somethings, are arguing with a woman who stands a short distance away. I'm immediately on high alert. She's younger, and I suspect she's either the boy's sister or maybe a young mother.

Seeing the tense situation worsening, I change direction. Ahead, the woman backs up from the men, scooping to lift the child into her arms. One of the men, lanky and wearing a green T-shirt, speaks harshly to her.

I'm nearly there when I hear the young woman say, "Tell him no. I don't need that kind of job."

"Come with us," Green Shirt says, reaching for her. "Why sit here begging for coins when we will provide?"

Fury steamrolls over my usual caution, and I slam straight into Green Shirt, shoving him so hard he falls to the ground. He darts back to his feet with a quickness that would be comical if it weren't so startling. He swings around, teeth bared.

Perhaps, I should've gone for subtle, but that's not how I operate when a child is involved. Still, though my training and skills mean I can take this man, I can't afford to fight him in public. Trying to regain my cover and my control, I state loudly, "Never let it be said that a nun doesn't know how to get a man's attention."

"Go back to God," Green Shirt hisses. Reaching into his pocket with that same alarming quickness, he pulls out a switchblade.

My training kicks in and with my own quickness, I capture his wrist and twist hard enough to bring him to his knees.

He cries out and drops the knife. It clatters onto the stones.

"Leave, go," his friend, a big nosed man with a sour mouth, says. Barreling toward my right side, I notice something in his hand. At first it looks like a retracted hiking stick, something he might've picked up at an outdoor store, but he extends with a snap, and I recognize what it is. It's a stun baton or shock stick. I'm familiar with them, have even handled them, used them. It's a useful tool containing twelve million volts of electricity that allows a person to attack or defend without getting too close to their target.

Well, this has escalated quickly. So much for Momma's notion that nuns are highly respected in the area. Obviously not a practicing Catholic.

Keenly aware of what's coming my way, I shove Green Shirt to the ground, side-step an angry swing of the buzzing baton, and nearly trip. Damn this tunic. Still, Baton Man's momentum works against him, and he lurches past me. My heart pounds frantically.

There's no room for nice here. Realizing I need to be quick and deadly, I turn, ready to unleash the beast. But a figure—huge biceps, veined forearms, broad shoulders, and a half-sleeve tattoo—jumps between me and my attacker.

Sean.

In a boxer's stance, Sean ducks the *whoosh* of the sizzling baton. He comes up under it, sends a devastating blow into Baton Man's big nose.

The crack is audible as the man's head snaps back. Blood rolls down from his nose and the split skin above it.

Baton Man isn't a fan of being punched in the face. Pinning his glare on Sean, he swings his weapon like a club.

"It's high voltage," I warn Sean, but I quickly realize my warning wasn't necessary.

Sean has this fight under control. His tight muscular form dodges and weaves, treating the buzzing weapon with considerable awareness as he slams Baton Man with a series of punishing blows.

Whoops. I forgot about Green Shirt.

Rising from the ground, he charges Sean from behind like he's about to take out a tackle dummy.

I hitch up my tunic and kick the back of Green Shirt's knee.

He drops to his shoulder, rolls, then springs back up like a kangaroo. He's certainly used to being knocked down. That's it. I'm done holding back. I shift to attack, bringing up my hands.

Sean beats me to it, slamming an open palm against Green Shirt's ear.

Green Shirt cries out, puts a hand over his ear, then pivots to Sean.

Knuckles bloody, Sean sends a perfect jab at Green Shirt's head.

Green Shirt dodges. He's very good at dodging.

The two men circle each other, avoiding Baton Man, who's out for the count and sprawled on the ground.

Sean delivers a series of blindingly quick, brutal, and effective strikes.

Green Shirt grunts with each hit. His eyes widen with surprise then fill with pain as the blows continue to land. Spitting out blood, he nearly dodges the last hit, but the quick strike skims along his jaw. With growing desperation, Green Shirt looks toward his switchblade.

"Not a step you want to take, lad," Sean says, his tone ice.

A whistle sounds from across the square.

Policia.

Green Shirt jolts, drops his hands, then runs over to his friend. He drags him up and they run. Well, Green Shirt runs. Baton Man grabs his weapon and kind of lopes after his buddy.

The officer dashes across the square, waving people who'd gathered to get out of his way as he charges after the men. Baton Man puts on a burst of speed, darting into a nearby alley.

There's a moment of settling tension, as everyone drawn to watch the fight realizes it's over. People drift off, some offering Sean praise, some calling me the Kung Fu Nun. This is not exactly the reputation I need.

As the last spectator leaves, I pocket the discarded knife. You never can tell when having a switchblade will come in handy. I then pick up the child's toy and bring it to him.

The boy's face is hidden in the shoulder of the woman holding him, so it takes a couple of moments of me whispering to him to get his attention. Finally, he lifts his head. My heart aches to see the tears streaking down his chubby red cheeks. He wipes at them, and his eyes go right to the toy.

I hand it to him with a smile. "It's okay. The men have gone."

Sniffling, he wraps his little arms around the toy and hugs it to his chest.

The woman holding him kisses away his tears. "Thank you for helping me and my son," she says to me and Sean, who's picking up his discarded flannel shirt.

I understand now why he wears that heavy shirt in this heat. Not concealed carry, he's covering his tattoo—a footballer kicking into a goal.

I need to tell him he's going about this covert work all wrong. He should play up his sport history, not hide it. It makes for such a tight cover: former footballer turned addict who disappears from the world and resurfaces in Mexico, trying to make a buck anyway he can. There's no link between him and the teen who was taken, so why try to hide something that requires less effort to use as cover? Armand obviously doesn't care to research, but if Sean ever gets in with Walid, he'll discover Sean's identity by running an image search.

I watch as he slips his glorious ink and large muscled biceps into the sleeves of his shirt. *Sigh*. Time to go back to being a nun. "Thanks for your help," I say, echoing the woman. "I wouldn't have wanted to release my jiujitsu on them."

Knuckles bloody, sweat soaking his shirt, a smile as pure and clean as sunlight, Sean chuckles a long, low laugh. The sound races along my skin, settling warmth in my stomach.

"Sister—"

"Dee."

"Dee. Certainly can't have martial arts nuns breaking assailants in half. Wouldn't be proper."

"No," I acknowledge. "It would start rumors and keep people up all night with worry."

Eyes still dancing, he says, "*Ach*, if they're anything like me, they already have a hard time sleeping since you arrived."

Oh?

Our gazes hold as his playful brown eyes smolder.

Remembering myself, I raise a brow.

His eyes widen. His mouth drops open. Patches of red rise up under his beard.

That's right, Sean. I'm still a nun. Well, as far as you know.

"Excuse me, Sister," he says.

"Thank you for your help, my child," I say, sounding and feeling like a pendeja.

Pushing my own idiota reaction and the desire that keeps rising in me down, I turn to the young woman watching us both with a confused expression.

Caught flirting with a Welshman when I'm undercover as a nun. Claro, not my finest hour.

Chapter 5

Sean

I'm a heathen. How did I become corrupt enough to make eyes at a woman of God? It's probably written on stone tablets near a burning bush—Thou Shalt Not Flirt with Nuns. Lord, forgive me. My only excuse is I keep forgetting she's a nun.

Especially here in the bright town square, moments after seeing said nun attempt to take on not one but two armed assailants.

Trying to resolve the conflicting natures of Sister Dee, I watch as she introduces us to the refugee woman. The woman, a girl really, answers with her name, Rosa Bella, and that of her tear-stained son, Carlos.

Dee picks up the woman's begging bowl. "Will you come with me to the soup kitchen? I can get you something to eat and maybe see if there's more we can do for you."

Rosa looks down and murmurs, "When we lived in Honduras, we didn't beg. My husband and I had a food cart, but things there became so bad, I had to leave after Pedro was killed by the gangs when he didn't give them money." She looks at her son, slung on one hip, clutching his toy, and swallows her obvious grief. "Without him there, they turned their eyes on me, so I sold the cart for this journey. Yesterday, I had my bag with all our money and our passports stolen, so now I can't even afford a place for us to sleep, and there are people here more dangerous than those we fled from."

A gnawing suspicion starts in my gut. I bet the men who offered her the job were also the blokes who'd stolen her bag.

There's no person more vulnerable than someone desperate for money with limited options.

"More dangerous?" Dee asks, eyeing the direction they ran off as if she'd like to hunt down the blokes. "Are they traffickers?"

Shaking her head, Rosa says, "Those men are headed north like me. They were paid by another to offer me a modeling job. They promised there would be no sex." She hitches a slipping Carlos back up onto her hip. "I don't believe them. I've heard stories of others who've taken El Rico Ladrón's modeling jobs and never come back."

"El Rico Ladrón?" Dee asks.

"These are old stories," I say, having heard of the Rich Thief before. "Rumors, tales used to explain women who've gone missing after being lured away by a man the locals dubbed El Rico Ladrón. They call these women *the disappeared.*"

Dee's lips thin out, grow tight. "Rosa, you should talk to the policia about—"

"No. Please, Sister," Rosa shakes her head. "I don't want trouble. I just want to get to safety."

After a moment's consideration, Dee gives a single firm nod. "Okay, but you must let me put you up at the hotel. At least until I can find a way to help you."

Rosa looks stunned by the offer. I'm a little shocked, too. No idea how much money nuns make, but can't be all that much.

"Sister, I can't let you pay my —"

Dee interrupts with a soft look, saying, "The order I'm with has money for these things. It won't be a problem, and this is, after all, the Lord's work."

Doesn't take much for the willful Sister Dee to convince Rosa. She might not like the charity, but she understands the danger for her and her son.

In quick order, we make our way across the square to the hotel.

"Give me a moment to secure the room," Dee says when we arrive.

Sweeping forward, she passes through the hotel's large black gates embedded in thick, sunrise-colored walls.

Rosa sits on a nearby bench, watching her son climb out of her lap and play with his little toy.

Having decided, I see my opportunity.

Trying not to let my size intimidate, I lean toward Rosa. "Are you headed to the U.S.?"

She shakes her head. "We're on our way to Canada. My cousin and her daughter have an apartment in Toronto. If I can get there, I can stay with her." She looks down for a moment and my throat fills with heat as I watch her fight back tears. "But the Canadian authorities won't let us in without our Honduran passports and getting replacements…" she shrugs, "it's very difficult."

I think of the journey and the miles through Central America and Mexico she's already come. The distance to Canada? Ach, breaks the heart.

Hoping not to offend her, I open my wallet and offer her what I have, along with a card that only has my cell number on it, no other information. I say, "Take this money and the card. I want to help you."

When she hesitates, I try to ease her worries. "I can replace the passports for you and your son."

Carlos hands her his toy and climbs back into her lap. She does an amazing job of juggling it all. "You can do that?"

"Yes. It's what I do." I don't tell her that I want to help her because I couldn't help Sofía. Unlike today, *that* fight I'd lost badly. Five against one; my odds hadn't been great. They could've just shot me, but were sending a message to any who might try to interfere with them.

"Why should I trust you?"

"Don't trust me. We can do the photos in an open place. No danger to you or Carlos. I promise."

Another second of hesitation, then she nods. Just in time.

"It's all arranged," Dee says, striding from the hotel with a squeak of the gate. "I'll show you to your room and speak with Sister Angelica about other ways we can help."

Rosa stands and picks up Carlos and his toy, which she hands to him when he makes grabby hands toward it. We walk inside together.

After we help Rosa and Carlos get settled, Dee and I return to the street. I'm planning on making my excuses when Dee turns to me. "Would my hero care to walk me to the soup kitchen?"

Hero? Pain stabs me in the chest. After Sofía, I feel like anything *but* a hero. "Oh, aye. But I probably protected those blokes from you more than you from them."

She smiles, and we move off. Leg screaming in pain after the fight, I limp more noticeably. Dee seems to take note, but doesn't mention it. Instead, speaking English with her light Spanish accent, she says, "What do you know of El Rico Ladrón?"

More than I'd like. "Locals speak of him as if he's in the past. Women were lured away through an invitation issued through others, then never came back. Were never heard from again. It's myth, really. Honestly, I think those lads threatening Rosa used the story as a cover for whatever they intended."

A line pinches the middle of her brow. "If this has been happening for years and it has nothing to do with traffickers, it could be…" She hesitates but finishes with, "A serial killer."

A chill works its way down my body. Not sure why I didn't see it before.

Something on my startled face must make her feel like explaining, because she does.

"Someone who consistently kills woman, who lures them using a predictable pattern—in this case, paying men who won't be around long enough to testify—and has done this long enough to have rumors circulating, to the point of garnering a name for himself… It's something to consider."

She's right. It's a wonder it never crossed my mind. "Where did you get your training, Sist… Dee?"

Eyebrows raising at the question, she gestures to my leg. "I recall reading about your injury. It was a bar fight, right?"

Tidy way of turning the tables and of pressing my buttons. I try to shake off the flash of annoyance, but I can't. I glance into the bright distance and the pink- and orange- and lime-painted buildings. A bar fight? Is that how people remember it? From most people, I wouldn't care, but her? "Do I look like the type to throw away my career on booze and anger?"

"No," she answers instantly. "You don't."

That soothes my wounded pride. "Thanks for that."

"Claro, what happened?"

There's a question. I don't answer as we pass trinket-sellers, food stalls, and people eating lunch by the fountain.

Where to start? Learning to walk again after the accident. Using drugs and alcohol to numb the pain. The long torturous road to mental and physical recovery? Ach, I shouldn't. It's a lovely day, too lovely to bring up ugly memories. Not right. "Too nice a day to get into all that."

"I could google it."

Bloody hell. "Didn't think you knew about google blackmail, Sister Dee."

"Just Dee. And I'm a nun, not someone from another planet."

Rubbing at the knot of pain forming at the top of my bum leg, I admit the truth. "I can't see you as a nun. Sorry."

There's a long beat of silence. I've offended her. I can tell by the way she's holding herself, but I have no idea how to take it back.

After a moment, she says, "Not a bar fight, so what happened?"

I like that, like how she moved past my offense. I like it enough that I tell her the truth. "I had an exhibition game in the States, then went out afterward to blow off steam. I was leaving the bar and saw one of my teammates, a guy known to have a temper, along with a morality problem, dragging a woman into his rental. Not a stretch to guess his intent. I ran over, punched him in the face, and tossed him to the ground. I was taking her inside to call the authorities, and—"

"He shot you in the leg three times."

"Aye." The papers had at least gotten that detail right. "Bloke who'd done it claimed self-defense. He wasn't prosecuted."

"The woman refused to testify?"

"He paid her off."

She frowns, a look that announces her disquiet and maybe even disgust. She's not the only one. I lost full use of my leg, my contract, but the lad who'd been about to kidnap and rape an innocent woman had lost nothing. He'd even gone on to have a magnificent career—only to revert to form. Years later, he was arrested for trying to rape a different woman.

We stop in front of the soup kitchen. People are lined up. The smell of beans and peppers fills the air.

As if she's used the silence to put the details together, Dee says, "The papers began to spin a different story. You went after him in a drunken rage. Him shooting you was self-defense."

"Team had to spin it that way or the squad would've lost two star players."

She grabs my hand, surprising me. Her hand is warm and soft.

I swallow.

She says, "They didn't have to. The fact that they would've lost games or money was no reason to lose their morals. You deserved better."

The warmth of her skin releases the knot of emotion in my throat, giving way to something else.

Gently, I pull my hand away.

Clenching and unclenching my damp palm, I tell her, "Next time we talk, I want to hear about you. About how you came to be a nun. Deal?"

A troubled expression crosses her lovely face. "That story would be filled with more errors than those articles written about you."

With that bit of makes-you-wonder, she turns and enters the soup kitchen.

Chapter 6

Dada

Seated on the floor of my sparse room at the convent, I wave my wrist—chipped with a security device and GPS tracker—over my laptop.

The computer beeps mechanically.

A moment more and I've entered a secure site on the dark web. I stare at a blue screen, until there's another beep and a box appears with my sister, Justice, inside.

A smile cracks her sharply angled face as she begins to laugh. "Do they make you wear that fucking hat in your sleep? The shower?"

I've gotten so used to the habit that I forgot I have it on. I click my teeth together and glare. Justice's Indigenous heritage has blessed her with the kind of regal beauty that makes her fierce and combative nature seem all the more incongruous.

Thankfully, she is most comfortable with someone who is blunt, and I'm happy to oblige. I'm nothing if not adaptable. "Laugh all you want, abrasive one, but remember I'm doing all of this for your mission."

"Testy," Justice says. "It's the celibacy thing, isn't it?"

She laughs at her own joke, but before I can respond, another box appears. Gracie. The side of her face and her red hair are the only thing visible as she focuses on one of the many computer screens in her office.

"Hey," Gracie says, finally looking at her central monitor. Her green eyes widen. Her hand comes up, smothering her laughter.

Joyous news. This is the way my night is going to go.

Tony pops on, chewing something he nearly spits out as his laughter booms over me like a car horn on full blast. His hazel eyes focus on the screen. "D," he says, wiping at tears running down his face. "You found it. The one cover ya can't pull off."

"There's a reason Momma only adopted two boys," I tell Tony.

Unbothered, he says, "All the male cool needed to balance out you twenty-six lame-o's."

Something about Tony's South Philly accent makes his humor hard to resist. My betraying mouth begins to give way.

I love these disrespectful people. In a family as big and complicated as ours—twenty-eight siblings adopted by one of the wealthiest women in the world—it made sense for Momma to divide us into groups based on our age, not when we were adopted.

It also made sense for running covert operations. These four are the siblings I've trained with, confided in, fought with, shared a hallway with in the Mantua Home, and ran secret operations with as an undercover agent.

"Would you all like time to get yourselves together?" I ask. "I can go get some tea and come back."

Slowly, they settle down, then each of our boxes shuffles right as another box opens.

Bridget's hair is a nest of strands stabbed with a comb on the side of her head. Her brown eyes appear sleepy under her glasses. She blinks, leans closer. A small smile lights her face. "I like your hat."

All four of my siblings burst into laughter, even Bridget, our resident yogi and all-around calm center trills out soft laughter.

Well, this is annoying.

A few more minutes of patience, patience that surely earns me sainthood, before I prod the group with, "Can we get to work?"

They calm down, and I quickly give them an overview of what's happened since coming to Mexico, including the chat with Rosa and my fear there might be a serial killer on the loose.

"So, this woman in the square," Tony says, causing the frame around his box to light up. "Someone offered her a job, and she said other women had accepted jobs then disappeared? Isn't that what traffickers do?"

"According to rumors and Rosa, it isn't traffickers. That's why I'd like to investigate."

Justice tilts her head. "Investigate what?"

Justice's tone says her patience is on a razor's edge. Pretty much where Justice's patience starts and ends, but especially with this mission—a mission to take down the men who killed her biological sister. We know each other well, my sister and I. Neither of us needs a fortune teller to see why I, someone stolen from her first home as a child, wants to explore what's happening to these women.

"I'd like to learn the truth," I say, laying it out there, daring her to challenge a side operation.

She does dare. "Well, fuck," Justice says. "If it has nothing to do with Walid, it'll have to wait until this op is over. We can't risk discovery right now, and you poking around, asking questions about missing women, is a time bomb."

"Asking questions is why I'm here. I can do both. Find out about Walid's security, the people around him, and research what's happening to these women."

"Not true. We need information on Walid," Justice says. "We need his routine, his likes and dislikes, info on his organization, his routes here, and specifics on how women are being secreted across North America."

I switch my gaze to each of my other siblings. "I call for a vote."

Dropping his head for a second, Tony clears his throat before looking back up. "Two things. First, you're our only operative in the area. Second, we can't take on every case. It's much safer for you to focus on the job at hand. You've got zero backup down there."

"Pero, zero backup is typically how undercover operations work, no?"

He rolls his eyes. "I vote no. Sorry, D."

Justice jumps in. "That's my vote, too."

"Me, too," Gracie says, and my heart sinks.

I spare Bridget the vote. "I'll respect the group decision, but if I happen upon any more information, I reserve the right to ask for reconsideration."

"Seconded," Tony says, and I breathe a sigh of relief.

I'm going to make sure I happen to come across that information.

Tony waves as if to scatter away the prior conversation. "Right now, let's focus on Juan, AKA Sean. Getting him in position with Walid so he's a proper asset is the key. Spend time with him every chance you can. Expose some part of you, feed him some truth, so he's more likely to trust you."

Expose myself? Feed him? *Yes. Please.* My belly flutters with an excitement that's as startling as it is unwelcome. This isn't a situation where I can afford to be sloppy. My cover is as good as any I've ever come across. People mostly ignore me. I can't risk being seen with Juan the Forger, a criminal, let alone flirting with him.

"You okay? Looking a little distracted," Tony says.

Uh. Tony. Stop being so observant.

"Leave her alone," Bridget says. "It's hard enough being on assignment and having women disappearing around you while researching a trafficker without getting teased."

God bless Bridget. Still, my other three siblings won't be put off with an admonishment. They're evaluating me now. Closely. Which means they require an answer.

What did Tony say about giving some truth? I sigh. "I'm having a difficult time finding my footing in this role, and it doesn't help that Sean is cute. *Very* cute."

"Uh oh," Gracie says "Stay clear of any complications. You know how that turns out for this family."

I do. Well, I know how badly it turned out for Gracie, whose former lover took everything that mattered from her—specifically her son—after finding out about our family.

"Not to worry," I tell my siblings, feeling on safer ground now that I've admitted the truth. "I take this mission as seriously as Justice does. I will not fail these women. All of you know that much about me."

Each of my beloved siblings nods in respect of this truth. Not only are we a family, we're a team. All of us have worked years to see this operation to this point. We will likely work another year before the final push.

It matters to us more than anything. All here have been rescued in one way or another. All here have given their lives to The Guild in place of any life outside it. And that makes us one, connected in a way that no one will ever be able to come between.

Chapter 7

Dada

The street on which I find Sean's apartment is shadowed and rundown—the exact place one would expect to find a document forger with a list of shady clients. Sean continues to impress me with what he's managed to do here as someone with no training. Still, excluding his fighting prowess, in many ways he's unequipped to deal with men as dangerous as Walid, and that's why Sean needs me.

With my tutelage, he'll be an unparalleled informant. But first, I need to do my own recon on him, find out what I can from his apartment while he's out. Perhaps, I can gain insight on how best to convince Sean to align with me. Since he's visiting the soup kitchen today, it's the perfect time to do my research.

I enter the three-story, white plaster building, smothering a yawn. Nun hours suck. The worst part is this city has so much to offer—museums, mole, fabulous restaurants, mezcal, clubs, and glorious sunshine that calls for a bikini.

It's all I can do to bend the rules enough to investigate without causing a stir with the other nuns who have no idea why I'm here. I've noticed more than one sidelong glance aimed at me as I shirk more and more responsibilities.

No one said undercover work made you popular.

The corridor inside Sean's apartment building smells of the dusty wooden stairwell, is dimly lit, and unexpectedly cool. Avoiding the stairs, I make my way down the hall to a pitted door marked by a sign that reads *Gerente*. Manager.

I rap lightly and after a few moments waiting, the door swings open. The smell of recently cooked peppers drifts out, and I look down at an elderly Mexican woman with silver hair and brown eyes, sitting in a wheelchair.

"Hello. My name is Sister Dee. Juan said you might be in need of some services, so I came to ask if there's anything I can do to help."

And to find out what you know about Juan AKA Sean.

The woman smiles up at me. "Hola, mi nombre es Sylvia."

Wheeling herself backward, Sylvia beckons me inside.

I follow her through a small apartment with many colorful Día de las Muertes figurines in different-sized glass cases and numerous bookshelves filled with books lining the walls.

She leads me into a pastel pink kitchen with lovely terra-cotta tiles.

I like her. Yes, that's based entirely on her decorating choices, ¿pero que mas necesito?

"¿Bebe cafés?" Sylvia asks.

I tell her I do drink coffee, and I notice the entire kitchen has been designed so she can work from her wheelchair.

I sit at the table, as there isn't a lot of operating space to begin with and the wheelchair makes it more so.

She fills a teapot, then turns a knob on the stovetop to heat the water. Grabbing the Café Bustelo and two cups, she tells me, "Juan is such a good boy."

I don't point out that he's a man because I'm sure, to Sylvia, a thirty-five-year-old man *is* a boy. At thirty-six, I feel I've earned the right to call myself a woman, but I don't balk when Momma calls me one of her girls. "How nice to have him here. You must get lonely."

Sylvia shakes her head. "Ay, no. I'm not alone, because my son is here."

"Your son?"

"That's me."

I startle as a man steps out from a door in the kitchen. I'd assumed that thin door was the pantry. A mistake I can't help but chastise myself for as the man whose blue overalls has a nametag that reads Geraldo moves farther into the kitchen. He's a big, tall and wide-shouldered—barely fits through that doorway into the kitchen. He leaves the door open behind him, and I look into a tidy and compact bedroom with a twin bed. How does he sleep in that?

"Hola," I say.

"¿Que es esto?" Geraldo responds.

What is this? A little rude, Geraldo, and a bit young to be this woman's son. He couldn't be older than twenty-four and has direct blue eyes with a skin tone much darker than Sylvia's lighter one.

Sylvia gently tells her son, "Sister is here to check on me."

Geraldo blinks and does a double take. His eyes widen. "Perdoname, Sister. I didn't see…" He trails off.

We stare at each other. Me because, coño, how did he not notice I'm a nun? After all, I'm wearing the full getup, habit and all. Will I ever get this right? "It's quite all right, my child," I say, feeling like an absolute fraud.

Nervously, he drags his hand up and down the front of his chest, then speaks slowly, as if searching for words. "I'm to fix the pipes in 4C."

With that announcement, he kisses his mother on the cheek and walks out.

Sylvia watches his retreating back and her eyes fill with love. She points to him. "Forgive him, Sister. He hurt his head years ago, but he is a good boy."

It sounds like Geraldo has had a hard life, but also continues to work hard to help his mother and to do his job. "You're lucky to be surrounded by so many good men," I say.

She smiles at me, then points to the ceiling, to Heaven. "The best one of all."

I smile back. This is the part of my job I love, meeting people who are full of joy for life. It's so necessary for me because, sometimes, in my world, it seems the bad guys are winning.

The teapot whistles, and Sylvia uses an oven mitt to grab the handle and pour the steaming water into two cups. Every part of me wants to get up and help, but her competence and delight in making the coffee is so obvious that I force myself sit still.

Turns out, with a little café in her, it's easy to get Sylvia to speak of Juan, to tell me his apartment number, to reveal he leaves early and comes home around one on Tuesdays. With my skills, it's going to be even easier to break into his apartment.

* * *

Sean's one-room apartment includes a kitchenette, breakfast bar with three barstools, a frameless bed on the floor in a corner, and lots of paint and paintings. There's barely a bit of empty wall showing with all the paintings in here. It smells like an artist's studio—brushes soaking, pencils and charcoals in metal tins, paint drying, crisp paper, and a touch of adhesive.

I'd known that Sean—for some reason, I can't mentally call him Juan anymore—painted. That's what he'd been doing in El Salvador. Still, it feels personal to see his artwork up close. It's so… revealing.

Taking time I really don't have, I walk around, admiring and touching things—his paint palette, his charcoals, easels, drawings, and paintings.

There's a lifelike painting of Sylvia on the wall that captures her spirit in the twinkle of her brown eyes, the laugh lines around her mouth, and the gleaming cross around her neck. Sean's talent is its own kind of magic.

Oh. I just love that bright pastel painting of the town with all the blues and pinks and greens. A magnificent artist, Sean uses sharp and exacting lines in his work. He has meticulous attention to detail and a penchant for drawing humans.

The slouching old men, youths who sit back on their heels

as if thrusting out their pelvis, and women with hips knocked to one side. I laugh, realizing he uses posture to convey character.

I stop by an etching still on the easel and nearly swallow my tongue. Although, at this point, it's only a sketch, and though he's never seen me in anything other than this drab tunic, I recognize the figure. Without touching, I run my fingers above the edges of a body he's gotten exactly right.

My body.

Swallowing my rising heart, I imagine his hand holding the pencil, imagine him tracing lines, mentally stroking my body.

Stop it.

Shaking myself, I drop my hand, then get down to more appropriate searching. Not difficult, really, because there's nothing hidden here. His one-room apartment includes art supplies and paintings and bags of stolen passports from all over the world. They're stacked on a wood drafting table, spread across his unmade bed, deposited on the breakfast bar by the kitchenette.

Along with the passports is the technical equipment to alter them—multiple tools for cutting and pasting, printing machines, blue lights, and lighted magnifying lenses.

What's this? I lift up the still drying Honduran passport and stare at the woman. *Rosa Bella* the passport reads. Sean made Rosa another passport? Illegal as anything… but also very sweet.

I scan the drying passports hung from a wire like a mini clothesline strung over the desk and spot another familiar face. Rosa's son. Sean has made a passport for him, too.

My throat grows tight. He's finding ways to ease the guilt of working undercover for a human trafficker in his attempt to rescue Sofía.

Not that I would know anything about that guilt. *Pero, no.*

I continue to walk the room, finding plane tickets stacked at the printer. Not just making passports. He's bought Rosa and Carlos airline tickets. There are other tickets. People I've seen at the soup kitchen. This is how he spends his money from Walid?

"Sister?"

"Ay!" Startled I swing around, dropping the printed-out tickets. To my horror, I find Sean squatting on the fire escape, staring at me through the window, his mouth set in a firm, disappointed line.

I bring a hand to my chest, mostly to buy time. "Dios. You scared the life out of me."

"Sorry about that, *Sister*." With alarming dexterity, he climbs in through the window. "Don't usually have guests break into my flat. Not sure of the protocols."

Hard to miss his sarcasm. "I didn't break in. The apartment was…"

He's shaking his head in outright disbelief. He knows I'm lying, and it's not hard to figure out why. The apartment couldn't have been left open if he'd gone out through the fire escape.

I turn back to the door and scan until I spot it. There's a small, nearly invisible device at the foot of the door. It must've registered me entering. I missed it, not only because it is so very tiny, but because it's very high-tech. I've underestimated this man.

I spin back around, smiling. "I need your help."

Wearing his trademark flannel, he swallows the distance between us with his sexy swaggering gate and says, "You broke into my flat because you need my help?"

I'm scrambling. My brain is scrambling. My heart is scrambling. He stops feet from me. I have to crane my neck, which is rare and uncomfortable.

I often wear heels in order to have the advantage of looking down on most men or meeting their eyes. My height has always given me a better sense of control and situational awareness.

Not having that advantage is supremely disconcerting. Not only that, but the heat of him rolls forward like lava, envelopes my staggering senses. He's put on a lot of muscle since he played. He's broader in the shoulders. Add his height to that and it's hard not to feel small.

I rarely feel small.

"Want to try the truth, luv?"

Luv? Not even *Sister* or *Dee*. I'm not on firm ground here. Maybe, I should switch tactics. What man doesn't like to have his ego stroked? Plus, I'd be a fool if I pretended I hadn't noticed the way he looks at me. The way he's looking at me right now.

"Help might be the wrong word." I make a point of running my tongue along my lips and am gratified when his eyes follow the movement. "I felt a strong need to be near you. With you."

Feminists everywhere are cringing at me using my sexuality to get out of this situation and, internally, so am I. Well, a little. He is so very hot that telling him what I feel, what I've kept hidden, is a bit of a relief.

"Really." He smirks, both interested and not buying it even a little. He leans closer. "Is that how you intend to play this?"

He smells so good, like freshly washed jeans and spring. Maybe he requires proof of my sincerity, a proof I am more than happy to provide. Quick as a hot second, I fist his T-shirt, tiptoe, and place my lips on his. Eager and hungry, I let go of all the tension of playing at being someone I'm not and let myself feel—really feel—the intense attraction I have to this man.

For a breathless moment, he freezes as my tongue plays along the seam of his mouth. But then, with a moan, he relents.

A bare moment of heat and naked desire rake painfully through every cell in my body as we grab each other, tongues intertwining, bodies screaming for more.

A flash, a millisecond of surrender that's so good, I'm consumed with my need for him, with getting closer to him.

I brush my hands down his chest, down and over his waist to his hard cock. It stands out under his jeans, firm and thick, and I rub the length of him. He moans, moves himself against my hand.

"Feels so good," he says.

It's going to feel a lot better. I start to unbutton him.

He grabs my hand, holds it there. His face a mask of pain, he whispers, "Please. You're not a nun. You don't kiss like a nun. Tell me the truth. I need to hear it."

The idea that he would be so consumed with the desire between us that he'd cross that line thrills me, and also fills me with guilt. Such is the life of an undercover agent.

Licking the taste of him, as sweet as any dessert, from my lips, I shake my head. "I can't absolve you or your sins. If that's what you're asking"

Cursing in Welsh, he pushes away from me, jumps back. "Oh, fuck. Sister. Sorry, I'm… I just…" He angles his head, squints at me and shakes his head as if reevaluating his apology. "Nah. No. I don't believe you're a nun. Not for a single moment."

Annoying. Am I losing my touch? "Why not?"

For a beat he stares at me, as if I can't be seriously asking that question right now. He looks away. "Other than you rescuing women and fighting blokes and breaking into my flat, and what your hands just did to me…" He gives a one-shouldered shrug. "It's, you know." He waves in my general direction.

Well, that's unhelpful. "Clarify, please."

He turns back to me, red sliding up under his beard and into his cheeks. "If you make me say it—"

"Say it."

"Surely, Dee, you've had men stare at you. You must've had people tell you. Surely, you realize how…"

People stare. Yes. But unless it seems a danger, I have no time to waste on looks. Still, it's obvious what he's getting at. It's insulting. I'm insulted for nuns everywhere. "Are you suggesting I'm too beautiful to be a nun?"

"Yes. No. I'm… It's not your beauty alone. It's… You give off a vibe, an energy. It's not the energy of a woman who spends a lot of time in prayer."

I'm giving off a non-nun vibe? Come on. That can't be my fault. "If my vibe isn't pious enough, doesn't that have more to do with the un-pious inner workings of your own mind?"

He bristles. "I didn't break into *your* flat, rifle through *your* things, and then give you the hottest kiss of your life. It's not me who has a piety issue. So, let's try again. Why are you here?"

Chapter 8

Sean

Standing in a room full of illegal documents passed to me by my industrious and not always above the law da, I find myself finally feeling like I've got the upper hand. Though I've only known her a few days, I've been off balance every time Dee and I've met. Honestly, I can barely breathe when she's near me.

Now, after her kissing me and copping a feel that has me as hard as I am certain she isn't a nun, I wait for her to convince me she is who she says she is.

"I told you why I came."

"Right. Sure." I stroll back to her. "Looking for a tumble? Okay. I'm your guy."

Let's see what she does with that.

Her eyes widen and travel the length of me. For a moment, I think I might have to put up or shut up. I'm finding I like that idea of putting up a lot.

She looks away, grasping the bracelet on her wrist. Pity, she's backing down.

I press my advantage. "Tell me why you're here,"

Her posture shifts so she stands with one hip slightly out. It's an I'm-taking-charge-of-this-situation posture. I know people, watch them and how they react down to the smallest detail. That, more than anything, has kept me safe here. And right now, that awareness screams at me that this woman won't admit the truth.

I get it. She can't trust me anymore than I can trust her.

She motions around the room. "Why are you helping Rosa and Carlos? Guilt?"

Guilt doesn't cover it. I feel sick to my stomach every time I'm asked to create a false identity for Walid or one of his goons. I tell myself they'd easily find someone else to do the work, but I also know that my skills are at a level few could manage to replicate. It's this level of skill, along with my da's help, that has allowed me to create a relationship with Armand, Walid's head of security.

I scrub a hand across my face. So much for feeling the tables turn. "Why would a man help people fleeing a desperate situation find safety? Seems obvious to me."

Her eyebrows draw in. "This is at odds with what your boss does. He takes advantage of the turmoil in these areas, ¿no?"

A lump erupts in my throat. "You break into my place, not a nun thing to do. Know who I work for, not very nun-like either. I don't need you to admit it to me, but I think it's becoming obvious you're working for some kind of government agency. Now, why don't you tell me the truth? You might be surprised to learn why I'm here."

She exhales a long, slow breath. "I know why you're here, Sean. You're here to find Sofía Hernández."

A bigger shock to my system might've been her throwing ice water down the front of my britches, but not by much. I take a step back, swing around as if to see if anyone heard her. No one here. It's okay. I check this place for bugs regularly. I'm careful. "How do you know that? Who do you work for?"

Although her eyes never stray from my face, she grasps that leather bracelet again. "I'm an undercover agent, part of the U.S. Catholic Working Group on Global Compacts on Refugees and Migration. The sisters here reached out for assistance, because they're worried about the refugees passing through the area. As Rosa said yesterday, some have gone missing. We are looking to discover how and put a halt to this."

Fury steamrolls across my shoulders. She's lying. Oh, she's a right good liar, but not good enough to get past me. "You're a spy? Sent by the Church to investigate the abuse of refugees? I'm supposed to believe this?"

Her shoulders straighten and she digs in her heels. "The Church has a long and deep history of helping refugees globally. If you doubt that nuns have a hand in that, that we do the difficult work, you need to go back and educate yourself about us."

I'm sure she's right. I'm absolutely sure there is some connection to truth here, but being a good liar with a good background story doesn't fool me.

"Okay, *Sister*. I still don't believe you." I put up a hand to stop her protest. "I don't need to believe. You know who I am. You could bribe or unmask me to Walid. But haven't. That's enough for me to let it be. For now."

I don't add that I figure one of the reasons she's not telling me the truth is because it's against protocols for whatever three-letter organization she works for. A look of relief crosses her face.

She takes in the room. "Where do you get these passports? They're from all over the world. Some don't even have stamps from Mexico, so you're not stealing them from here."

A clever lady, who can turn a conversation on a dime. She's back on the offensive.

I pick up a passport, the one for Carlos, and brush it off. "You have your secrets. I have mine."

Her gaze drops to the passport. "I can see you care, Sean."

I flinch on hearing her speak my name.

"I respect you for that. I also see you're beginning to realize how fruitless your quest has been."

She gives me the silent opening to object. I can't. I've recently begun to doubt my methods, despite the information I've gathered. I need to get closer to Walid but have no idea how to do that. Armand keeps me at arm's length.

"If you team up with me, I can help you find Sofia."

My heart thumps hard against my chest. "You can do that? Find Sofia?"

"The people I work for have already begun mapping routes through the US, but we need more."

This sets my heart racing. I want so badly to trust this

woman, to know there is someone with enough government connections to be capable of acting on what I've discovered already. "How can you help me find Sofía?"

For a moment, it seems she's almost disappointed with my reply, as if she'd hoped I wouldn't agree, but she blinks and says, "First, if you help me, you have to promise to follow my instructions down to the letter, because this endeavor is very dangerous."

My wounded pride nearly makes me object. Instead, I say, "Give me the details."

"I need insights into Walid's business, his personal habits, his compound security, his moods, his personnel, his layout, especially of the mines he has underground at his compound."

"He has underground mines? Why in hell would he ever tell me?"

"Some, he'll tell you. Some, others will tell you when you begin working at the compound. Some, you'll be able to infer. Some, you'll have to take risks to uncover. Specifically, you'll have to get into his computers. It's dangerous work, Sean. Dangerous enough that if it didn't mean the freedom of many women, including your Sofía, I wouldn't ask for your help."

"I've no idea why you think he'd invite me to work at his compound."

"You're going to offer him something he wants."

I can only imagine what that git wants. Makes the stomach turn.

I don't say that, but she must read the disgust in my face, because she says, "I can tell you his motivations, what he wants, and how to offer him something that will repress his suspicion, even when he finds out who you really are."

My mouth slams shut. My teeth grind together. "Are you threatening me?"

She rolls her eyes. "No. I'm telling you that in order to get closer to Walid—seeing as you haven't done the hard work of cementing a false identity—you're going to have to accept that he's going to figure out who you are. When he does, you'll have a story that enables him to accept you, a story that will make your offer to him one he can easily accept and believe."

"What am I going to offer him?"

She smiles softly at me. "So, will you work with me?"

"Let me get this straight, all you need me to do is take down someone I'm already trying to take down, and you'll help me find and rescue Sofía?"

"Exactamente."

She's got to be working for the feds. Has to be. *Bollocks*. What choice do I have? "Right. I'm in."

Chapter 9

Sean

I've got a bad feeling. Though the bank-sized safe, the table Armand and I sit at, and the two guards flanking the door barely dent this large room, it feels too full. Tension beats in every corner, nearly drowning out the late-night revelry in the bar below. The pulse in my ears pounds out both fear and loathing.

In my quest to find Sofía, I've met a lot of men who have given me the creeps or made me feel like beating the spit out of them. But I've never met anyone I detested as completely as Armand Stoker.

A total nut, he's right good with anger, hatred, jealousy—any emotion other than happiness, which he labels a weakness. That's why I never smile in his presence. That and I'd like to punch him in the face. Still, this man has gotten me closer to finding Sofía than I could've gotten on my own. Not that he's aware of it. If he were, I'd be dead.

Getting dead is always a possibility. The guards, the message Armand is sending with them, is something I need to explore. I sneer at the men by the exit. "Usually when I deliver, those blokes stay outside."

The *flick, flick* of steel against Armand's dry cuticles echoes across the cavernous space. He shrugs. "What does it matter? We are speaking English."

My flesh crawls at his non-answer. I don't glance down at my cell, which is off and placed on the table. Dee hid a tiny device on it. She said even with my cell turned off the device could capture content from any nearby cell phone. Armand's cell sits on the desk as well.

If he knew about that device, it'd be bad. Armand's appearance—his crooked nose and caved-in right cheek—tell a story, and it's not the story of a bloke who shuns violence.

I evaluate the guards more closely. Growing up, if I wasn't on the pitch, I was in the ring. These men got weight, but I could take them. Well, I could if they weren't armed.

Knowing who makes decisions for Armand, I press my only advantage, "Is Walid unhappy with my work?"

His lips firm. "No."

That's good. It means he's not likely to make any move against me that would require him answering to Walid. He slides the envelope containing the most recent request from Walid across the table. Documents for his brother Aamir.

I've moved up in the world. I'm not only creating documents for Walid, but for his brother and their extensive network overseas. Makes me sick.

Got to keep reminding myself I'm collecting enough information to bring them all down. Thanks to Dee that end seems closer than ever.

Armand doesn't open the envelope. At this point, he knows my work is perfect. I speak up, taking control as Dee instructed. "When you deliver this lot, I'd like you to tell Walid I want a meeting. I've gained access to materials that'll allow me to create border cards, easier to use and cheaper to produce, not just for his men." I swallow panic, remember that Dee knows what she's doing and say, "But for the women."

He pauses, meets my eyes. I have his interest… or is it his anger?

"Why should I help you when you are making my job more difficult?"

"Am I?"

"You took up the cause of nuns, rescuing women who were not yours to rescue."

Startled, I struggle for an answer. I know what he's referencing and everything in me wants to go to battle for Dee and Rosa, tell him to back the fuck off, but to do that is to squander opportunity.

"Thought Walid didn't snatch women from town because of the cartels."

Armand's eyes become slits. "Why do you keep meeting with her, the nun? I saw you before…" He halts with his nail file paused over another cuticle. "Leave it to you to find the one fuckable nun in the soup kitchen."

I nearly dive over the table and beat the ugly out of the bastard, but I don't because I've learned to control those impulses. They happen fairly regularly when dealing with this kind of degenerate.

I do remember seeing him when I'd first met Dee. His eyes had been as aggressive as fire.

Does he suspect her? And now me since he's seen us together twice? No. If he suspected, he'd take me to Walid.

It seems a bit of a coincidence, though, that he's seen me twice with Dee. Was he in the area? Or is he having me followed? Neither seems likely. That leads me to wonder… and here's a disturbing thought… could Armand have hired the two men to go after Rosa? Is Armand El Rico Ladrón?

Alarm settles in my gut. If Dee is right and there *is* a serial killer, it could be Armand. Wouldn't put anything past him. Before Walid, he worked for the cartels. He's had powerful contacts in the area for decades, but no real power of his own, no real business of his own. Man is angry and violent and as invisible as one can get while still being knee-deep in some of the dirtiest shite out there.

What could he get away with if he wanted?

"What's this about? Surely one nun can't warrant so much attention from you."

"Nun." He snorts in disgust. "She looks like a whore to me."

Anger snakes over my skin, raising the hair on my arms and

neck. I play it as cool as I can with my gut churning and my fists clenched. "Whore, nun, makes no difference to me." The words nearly dry up in my throat as my stomach turns over. "You want me to stay away from her, no worries."

If it'd keep her from Armand's mind, I'd stay a mile from Dee. But it won't so I need to be very careful when I do meet her.

Armand stops digging at his nails. The room goes so quiet I can hear the pounding base from the club downstairs and nearly the sound of the muscle ticking in Armand's jaw before he lurches forward.

"To be clear, I want you to stay away from her and any woman in town who could make you hard. The rest, you can have."

Clear enough. "Right. No worries. How about that meeting?"

Armand lets out a long low breath, seemingly satisfied with me backing down.

For my part, I can't bring this fucker and his boss down fast and hard enough.

Armand nods. "I'll arrange your meeting. Tell me more about the border cards."

He wants to take credit. Fine by me. The goal is the goal. But I damn sure can't wait to get to the heavy bag in my building's basement and pound on it like it was Armand's face.

Chapter 10

Dada

After a long and grueling lunch crowd, the soup kitchen finally slows down and the cafeteria begins to empty of people and noise. I grab a rag and wipe splatters from around the food well, as the other sisters also start to clean up.

My exhausted mind drifts to Sean Bradford and the details on Walid he's provided. It's a gold mine. Because of what he's shared, my unit is working on moving up the timeline for taking out Walid and his brother. To think years of planning could all come to fruition by year's end has me nearly giddy.

I need more time to research what he's brought us, but a new group of refugees has come through, flooding the town with new mouths to feed and new stories to hear. I've barely had a moment these last few days, but even with all the activity, it hasn't escaped my notice that Rosa hasn't shown with Carlos today.

A thread of unease slides into my chest and grabs my attention. This feeling isn't something I can ignore. I don't ignore my instincts. I need to check on Rosa and Carlos.

Turning to Sister Lupe I ask, "Have you seen Rosa today?"

Lifting a tray from the food well with a set of tongs, she shakes her head. "No." She shrugs. "She's probably continued her journey north."

"No, she hasn't." I would know. "And she wouldn't skip lunch, because she has a small child to feed."

"Perhaps the child is sick."

Maybe. I put away the washcloth. "I'm going to check on her, to make sure. Do you think anyone will mind?"

Sister Lupe drops the tray with a clang, spilling water across the area I just cleaned. "*I* mind. You have been shirking your duties, and though Sister Angelica gives you leave to do so, I am not her. You will stay and do your job."

Praying for patience, recognizing the difficulty in putting together a new undercover identity, I bite my tongue, nod respectfully, and keep working.

Sister Lupe picks up the tray and moves off, and I watch as she exits into the back. The kitchen door swings closed.

I take off.

The day is mild and sunny as I make my way out of the soup kitchen and down the street. My feet slap the concrete as I move with haste, and though it's a short distance to Rosa's hotel, I can't help the mounting fear.

Inside the hotel, I walk-run across elaborate orange-and-blue tiles to the front desk.

"Sister Dee." The manager smiles.

Though my stomach is turning, I smile back. "I lost my keycard to Rosa's room. Can you replace it?" The truth is I never thought to keep one.

"Of course, of course," he says, quickly making a keycard for me.

As calm as if this were all routine, I take it, smile, then hustle down the hall to Rosa's first floor room.

I knock on her door. No answer. Removing a small .22 from my thigh holster, I flick off the safety, tap the keycard, then enter. Though the bed's unmade, the room is clean. There's no signs of a struggle. I sweep and clear the room, the bathroom, then go for the closet.

Something rustles inside. I know before I open the door who I'm going to find. I can hear his muffled sobs. Putting the gun away, I slide the door open and drop to my knees.

My heart breaks as Carlos rushes for me. Repressing my own cry, I grab the sobbing child in my arms and hold him tight, tight enough to convince him he's safe. He buries himself against my body and his tears quickly soak through my tunic.

I rock him, offering him as much comfort as I can in this moment of sadness and regret. This is my fault for not pursuing El Rico. I was slow to act when I knew better, when fate presented me with the opportunity to help others. I let my family, who aren't on the ground here, who didn't come face-to-face with Rosa, make the call for me.

No more.

Carrying the shaking child out of the room and through the lobby, I tell the manager to call the policia, and then I ring the abbess and tell her I need her help at the hotel.

Waiting for them, I sit on a chair in the lobby and whisper soothing words in Carlos's ear as I stroke his back. In my heart, I gather every last bit of determination to find Rosa and bring her home safely to her son.

* * *

An hour after an exhausted Carlos has been taken to a loving couple in town, the hotel lobby is overrun with policia and my temper is fraying. I thoroughly dislike Comandante Javier Lopez.

"You see, my dear," Javier says, "many women leave their children, so you are wasting your time. Go back and pray, Sister, and leave the investigations to us." Dark hair, dark sunglasses—worn inside for some reason—and a half-foot shorter than me, his tone still tries to pat me on the head.

"Rosa didn't leave her son, Comandante. She was taken."

He waves away an approaching officer. "Her room is clean and nothing was taken. You are jumping to conclusions."

Straightening my spine, willing myself not to seek the comfort of the bracelet on my wrist, I employ a tone of brisk frustration. "You're the one jumping to conclusions. Rosa didn't abandon her child."

The comandante shrugs. "My experience tells me otherwise, but you have a too-kind heart. I know the cold realities of this journey, of traveling to El Norte, because I've seen it before. You think she is the first woman to leave her child?"

My fear and anxiety are morphing into stomach-turning rage. This man isn't going to even *try* to find Rosa. Hadn't tried to find the women who'd gone missing in the past. Won't try to find any that go missing in the future.

Of course, I know the statistics. Due to the horrible drug wars, drugs many in my country crave, ninety-three percent of crimes in Mexico go unsolved. Those are just the *reported* crimes.

Logic and self-preservation tell me not to push. My "too-kind heart" knows pushing won't bring lost women home, and the last thing I need is to make a name for myself when I'm undercover on a separate assignment and yet… "If you never search, how can you know they've left their children? How can you know they weren't taken?"

A disturbed frown etches lines around his full chin, reminding me of a puppet. "You live an entirely different life from these people. From us. You are sheltered, taken care of. You don't know what you're talking about. The rules here aren't made by God, Sister. They're made by men."

With that, he lifts his sunglasses and stares at me with mean brown eyes. "Men like me."

For a moment, his statement looms between us, as solid and immovable as the bars of a prison. I could continue to challenge him, but to what end? It would only serve to draw me more surely under his scrutiny and won't satisfy my anger or growing suspicion of him.

Adopting the same confident calm I've seen Sister Angelica wear, I turn with a, "God sees all, Comandante."

From behind, Javier whispers, "It seems to me that He must be blind."

Chapter 11

Sean

Seated at my drafting table, eyes tired and sore, I check every detail, down to the smallest watermark. The passport is finally perfect.

My cell buzzes. Reaching into my pocket, I answer, "Oi."

"She's gone," Dee says.

Leaning back, I grip the phone tight. "What are you on about?"

"I think Rosa's been disappeared. She wasn't in her room, and Carlos was hiding in the closet."

A knot forms in my throat. I drop Rosa's passport, slide off the seat, and begin to pace. "Is he okay?"

"He's safe. The sisters found a good family in town to care for him until his mother is located. Unfortunately, he wasn't unable to give us any information."

"Do the policia have leads?"

A sound as much fury as frustration rolls through the line. "I spoke with a Comandante Javier, and he believes she abandoned Carlos, but *I* believe he makes broad assumptions."

A floorboard cracks under my pacing feet. "I know of him. A few years ago, the fiancée of the bloke whose mum owns this building went missing and the comandante was all too quick to look for a scapegoat."

"Do you mean Geraldo?"

Of course she's already met Geraldo. In the week she's been teaching me to be a proper spy, I've learned she doesn't miss a trick. "Aye. Geraldo. He was the first person to tell me of El Rico Ládron.

Also said that, when his fiancée went missing, the comandante blamed him, tried to pin him for her disappearance. Frustrated and trying to clear his name, Geraldo did his own investigation. No one knows exactly what happened, but they found him with his skull smashed in. Lad was weeks in hospital. Never been the same."

"Pobrecito. I spoke with him and…" She pauses as if searching for the right words. "How much does he understand?"

"He's as sharp as a knife." Especially when it comes to mechanical stuff.

"Do you think he could have information for us? Maybe whoever took his fiancée took Rosa?"

Rubbing the scruff on my jaw, I catch sight of one of my recent paintings. Dee and Rosa walking across the town square and into a beautiful sunset with Carlos following. I clear my throat. "I'll ask. But he forgets much of that night. Hate to trigger bad memories for nothing."

"I understand, but he's our only lead right now. He and El Rico, and I've already begun asking around after him. I'm in the square now, speaking with refugees."

"Alone at night? When a woman has gone missing?"

"I can take care of myself. Kung Fu Nun, remember?"

Ach, she's right. She's taught me a few good tricks this week. Subtle ways to end a fight. Not the fists and fury I've used my whole life. Still… "Right, I'll go talk to Geraldo now. Let's meet after. Someplace safe and isolated. You give me the questions, so I can interview people. They might respond better to Juan the Forger than Dee the Nun."

Another pause. Longer. "I should've thought of that. I should change."

"Change?"

"Call me after you speak with Geraldo. We can decide where to meet."

She hangs up before I can respond.

Bugger.

#

Of course, my bum legs decides tonight is the night it's going to remind me how shite it is.

Sounding like Captain Hook working his way across the bow of the *Sea Devil*, I clomp down my building's stairs.

Hitting the last step, I see a figure move in the shadows—a corner that should be lit.

Shifting feet, I raise my hands.

Geraldo comes out, carrying a screwdriver and a lightbulb.

I stagger, then put a hand to my heart. "Mate, you gave me a start. Why're you lurking in corners?"

With a frown that cast doubt on my powers of observation, Geraldo holds up his lightbulb. "Light's out."

I give him a pass for the heart attack. "Glad you're out here. Was going to knock, but hated to bother your mum during her telenovela."

Geraldo's mouth twitches. "It's not wise."

"Exactly my thinking." *And* that I didn't want to upset Sylvia with talk of her son's missing fiancée. Sylvia had been there the night Geraldo first told me of his fiancée. She'd helped her son fill in a lot of the details. It had been a heartbreaking evening. "I'm on my way out. Walk me to my car?"

Surprise on his face, Geraldo looks at the dark corner and then at the lightbulb, obviously worried about leaving it dim in here

"It's important."

With a nod, he puts bulb and screwdriver into a toolkit, then shoves his hands into the pockets of his coveralls. "Sí. Rápido."

Man takes his job seriously. Has since I met him on the day I arrived in Oaxaca. Me, literally a homeless person. Despite his speech issues, Geraldo struck up a conversation with me. Finding a room to rent and a friend had been that easy.

Outside, the streets are dark and moderately busy. Geraldo keeps pace with me easily enough, but I can feel his tension. Or maybe he can feel my tension and that's fueling his.

Ach. Like a bat to the Devil, best be fast. "I was talking to Sister Dee today."

Geraldo's brown skin turns russet, and he lowers his head as we swing around the building to where I'd parked on the street.

"Doesn't look like a nun."

"Glad I'm not the only one who thinks so, but, trust me, don't say it out loud. Hugely offensive."

Geraldo's eyes go wide. "You didn't."

"Ach, she was so lush I couldn't help it. The words slipped past my lips before I could retrieve them."

Not the only thing to slip past my lips when it comes to her.

Grinning, Geraldo nods. Feels good to be understood. And he does understand me. We get along easily, work out regularly in the basement—I'd been thrilled to find he had a bag setup. Sure, communication isn't in his Strengths column, but running full out is no longer in mine.

It's best to be direct with him; cuts down on the back-and-forth. "Sister Dee told me a refugee woman has been taken from her room."

Geraldo hisses through his teeth, a sound a man recently punched in the gut might make.

My own stomach tightens. "Sorry, mate. Can't be easy on you. I know you don't remember much about your investigation into your fiancée…"

Geraldo's ham fist comes up to knock on his own head. "Not in there."

Poor bloke. "Anything you can remember about her disappearance, even something before the"—*accident* isn't the right word to describe what happened to him—"incident could help."

I take out my key as we stand beside my lime-green Cadillac, a smuggling vehicle I got for next to nothing. Like everything in my life these days, it walks back and forth over the line between legal and illegal.

Squeezing his eyes closed, Geraldo goes still for a long moment. A single tear trails down his cheek.

I reach out and pat his shoulder.

His eyes pop open and pin me. He remembers something.

He gropes the pocket on his coveralls, then takes out the small pen and notepad he carries. Helps with communication.

He writes a series of numbers.

I know immediately what they are. “GPS coordinates?”

Geraldo points with a dirt-encrusted finger. “I remember. This.” He taps the note. “Kept repeating… I woke… at hospital.” He tosses his head to the night sky and groans in deep frustration. “Policia looked. Nada. Looked myself, dozen times.”

“Is this where you were found?”

He shakes his head.

“Not where you’d been found, but something you remembered from that night?”

He nods.

“And you’ve checked this area at least a dozen times before?”

“Aye.”

“Oh, *aye*, is it?” Can’t help the grin. “We’ll make a Welshman of you yet.”

“*Bugger*, not likely.”

I full-out laugh. “You’re a clever one.” And he knows the area. If he couldn’t find anything, it seems a dead end. Still, I take the paper. “Thanks, mate. Take it easy.”

As I turn to go, Geraldo grabs my arm, the warmth in his blue eyes ice cold. “Careful. Dangerous.”

A flush of cold energy works its way down my spine, setting the hair at my neck flying. “Will do. No worries.”

Chapter 12
Armand

I drag the girl down the basement stairs. The puta fights like a panther. She swings at me, misses, tries again, and scratches my arm with her long, dirty nails.

"Let me go!" she screams. "My son needs me!"

"He doesn't need a whore," I tell her, kicking her legs out from under her and letting her roll the rest of the way into the basement.

At the bottom of the stairs, she tries to crawl away. I jump down and grab her, drag her across the room by her hair.

Her gaze takes in the room with the metal chains embedded in the walls, the bloody mattresses, the knives, the drill. Her eyes widen and fill with terror. "What is this place?"

"It's a meat locker, puta," I tell her, grabbing her face and squeezing. "If you didn't look just like her, I'd show you how it works."

She stops. Her brow furrows. "You took me because I look like another?"

"The accident of your birth." I unlock the chains, bring them to her wrists. "Like mine, like all of us. It defines the destiny of every person on this planet. Though some would tell you otherwise… but they lie."

She slaps me. "Let me go. Please. My son. He is alone."

"Alone? You let a whore buy you a room. Let her take care of him."

She kicks out at me with her unchained leg. "She is no whore!"

I hit her in the nose and she cries out, quickly bringing her hands up to protect herself by covering her face. As if she could escape her punishment that easily.

I punch through her hands again and again. “Your room was paid for by a whore and with whore’s money.”

It feels so good to hurt her, to hit her, to let her know that my strength is mightier than her filth. The blood and her muffled cries send desire surging through me. It wouldn’t be the first lamb meant for slaughter I gorged myself upon, but this one is needed to save my life.

Remembering this, I pull back from hitting her and watch as deep red blood drips through the gaps in her fingers. Her broken hands drop from her face. She’s unconscious. I spit on her, then handcuff her to a water pipe.

What a mess.

I check her pulse. Still alive.

Coño, there’s blood on my pants. Still angry, I pull out my phone. I’d hoped to get rid of this woman tonight, but now… look at hcr.

I text Walid to let him know his “merchandise” has been found and that it will be shipped to his buyer in a week.

Thc tcxt comcs back. “Two days.”

I sigh and stare at the blood-stained woman. “I hope you’re a quick healer.”

Blood trickles from her silent mouth. It would’ve been so much easier if she hadn’t fought.

Chapter 13

Sean

It's full dark when I pull up to the street corner where I'm to meet Dee. I put my car in park and watch as the traffic light at the corner turns green.

Dee's nowhere in sight. Don't know her that well, but she's not been late before. Plus, she knows the importance of this. After I phoned her about Geraldo's coordinates, we changed plans. We're no longer asking around for information on Rosa. We're going to check the location out.

I scan the area again. A long-legged woman in black—cargos, army boots, bomber jacket, and knit hat—straightens from a lean against the traffic post. She's hot enough to make me do a double and triple take.

Wait one holy minute. No.

She walks forward. Oh. Good. Lord. It *is*. The richness of her skin, the sway of those hips, the length of those legs, long enough to wrap… Sister Dee.

Fine then, the Devil wins. If I'm to resist her, I'd rather choose Hell.

She walks around the car, knocks on my window.

Swallowing my very inappropriate declaration—and my tongue—I lower the window. She leans in, bringing all that lushness along with the scent of rose water.

Honey-brown eyes twinkle with her smile. Those eyes. A man could get lost in them.

"A lime-green Cadillac… such a lovely car color."

Grinning like an idiot, I nod because the thing in my throat that's supposed to operate airflow so I can utter words has blocked up completely.

She gestures at the car. "Can I come inside?"

Fuck. The door, mate.

Mouth still seeking air, I hit the unlock button.

With a jaunty walk, she goes around the front, slides into her seat with one long leg leading the way, then throws her backpack onto the floor.

Gah. Can't get over it. I thought she was beautiful in her habit, but that getup dulled her. As had her contacts. "Your real eyes are lovely."

Reaching up, she removes the hat from her head. "Thanks. I'm surprised you didn't assume these are contacts and the brown is my real eye color."

"There's no mistaken those are real. You shine, luv."

Gah. I'm gushin' over her. In my defense, it's the first time I've seen all of her, including her hair, which is shorn tight against her scalp. *Elegant* comes to mind. My hand itches to run along the edges of her face, her perfect ear, her beautiful jaw.

If we weren't living through this hell, it would be different. *We* could be different. Got to remember I'm just her informant and the bloke helping her find a missing woman.

Looking away, I slip into drive and pull onto the road. "The GPS coordinates are over an hour away…" can't help the sour, "*Sister*."

"Dee."

"For a nun, you sure don't like to be called Sister."

Her fingers move to the leather bracelet on her wrist. "Thanks for the suggestion of changing my outfit."

Wasn't really my suggestion, but I like that she didn't deny what I know is the truth. "You wear it well. Seems more natural than your tunic."

"Sean."

There's soft warning in her voice, but I find I'm not interested in her threats or disapproval. I want her truth.

Nearly missing the turn—the streets aren't well lit or well-maintained—I hit the brakes, jerk the wheel, then make the right.

Dee slides in her seat.

I don't apologize. I'm finding I'm unreasonably angry. Keyed up, actually. "I researched the nun group you claim to be from, and though it's on the fringes of possible, it's also highly unlikely."

Exhaling a long, low breath, she says, "Do you remember what you told me the day we met when I called you Sean on the street?"

"Aye. I said I couldn't be that man, not here."

"And I said I'd keep your secret." She turns and looks at me. "I have. Now, I'm asking you to please stop questioning me about things I can't give you the answers to."

She *can't* answer, not *won't*. That makes a difference. Somehow, makes me feel better. Proof that whoever she works for wouldn't like her spilling the beans.

I nod. "As long as we both know I'm not the only one playing a role, I'm good with it."

She doesn't nod, doesn't agree, but her eyes dip closed for one second before she turns forward again in her seat.

Feeling like we're making progress, I head toward the four-hundred-acre property Geraldo's coordinates fall in the middle of.

Chapter 14

Dada

It's nearly midnight and the only lights on this dark, desert road are the ones from Sean's car. There's a rough chill coming through the vibrating window. The car smells of leather seats, cool desert, and gorgeous man. Sean and I have barely spoken since our initial conversation when I got into his car. It's my fault.

I'm off my game. I've never told an informant as much as I've revealed to Sean tonight. Even though I walked the line of not saying it directly, it was obvious to us both what I meant. The thing is, I'm glad I told him.

He's risking so much to help so many people, and the only thing he's asked for is the truth from me. I've done what I could, but I wish I could do more.

Sean pulls over on the side of the dirt road and parks overtop of scrub and brush. It's a smart move. We haven't seen any cars along the ride, but the roadway is unlit and compact enough that, if he hadn't pulled over this far, someone could've sideswiped his car.

"This is it," he says. "Can't get closer to the coordinates in this thing. It might be pretty, but this old Cadillac can't make it over all that brush and large stones."

"I'm prepared," I say, pulling up my backpack. "I have water, flashlights, equipment, and nutrient bars."

He grunts with what I take as approval. It's not always easy to decipher the subtle differences in his nonverbal responses. Well, some of them. There are those that are unmistakable, like the soft way he moaned into my mouth the first time he kissed me.

Reaching into my bag, I take out my extra Glock, run through a quick series of instructions, and offer it to him. His hands go tight on the wheel.

He shakes his head. “I’ll not be carrying that.”

“But—”

“No, luv. Put it away. I won’t touch that thing.”

My eyes drop to his leg, his injury. Of course. I’m so insensitive. I put the weapon back into my bag. “I’m sorry. I hadn’t considered.”

“Don’t consider it. Please. Don’t.”

That’s the first I’ve heard real anger from him—or is it frustration? I know so much of his history but am still learning his moods. He knows even less of me, who I really am.

I draw in a breath at a sudden thought, a small wonderous realization. I can tell him something of me and of him. “Do you remember that game in the FAA Cup when you scored three goals and single-handedly defeated a team in the Premiere League?”

An uncontrollable smile rolls across his mouth. “Best game of my life.”

I smile back, pin him with my gaze so he knows how much I mean what I’m about to say. “I watched the whole thing online. Me, cross-legged on my bed, laptop in front of me, a pillow hugged to my chest, and…” I lick my lips. “It was so early in the morning, I kept burying my mouth into my pillow, biting it, screaming into it while I watched you so I wouldn’t wake anyone. You were so beautiful.

“The way you slashed madly down the pitch, glided and spun and scored. It captured me. When the game was over, I was shaking. It seemed my heart was full and broken all at once. Full of joy and broken, because I never thought to see the likes of that stunning performance again.”

His eyes don’t stray from mine. I feel as if, for the first time, he is *really* seeing me, seeing my truth. “But then, years later, you walked into a soup kitchen, and my heart leapt, and everything I had felt that day happened all over again, and my heart was full and broken all at the same time.”

"Ach," he growls out, and it sounds constricted and tight and this time, it's all he needs to say.

I know he gets the fact that I see him. To me, there is no difference in Sean sprinting with all his pre-injury skills down the pitch or limping down the cafeteria line waiting to be served free food.

Of course, there's so much more to him than either scenario can capture: the lion heart of him that puts his body on the line to help others now, as much as he did then for his team, the humor and passion, the artist and protector.

After another moment, he reaches out, then runs a hand down the side of my face.

I lean into him, wanting his warm touch more than I can say.

He whispers, "When you asked why I don't see you as a nun, I had tidy answers. None true." He takes a deep breath in and exhales it out.

I put my hand atop his large one, pressing both to my face and feeling our deep connection radiate warmth through my skin.

He says, "But the truth was—is—I can't see you as a nun because that's a role, an identity that slips from my eyes every time I look at you. You're fire and grace, intelligence and wit, black and beautiful, sexy and determined, gentle and fierce. And it doesn't matter what costume you put on, what's on your head, hands, or feet, I'll always see that truth when I look at you."

I lean toward him.

He rushes forward and his lips meet mine in a wild joining that explodes into an instant intense throwing-caution-to-the-wind kiss.

Oh, and can the man kiss. I'm lost to the pull of his lips, strong and soft. The smell of him, masculine and natural. The heat of him, pressing against me. The heavy tangle of our breaths, the magnetic pull of our bodies. I want him in an aching, heavy way.

A coyote howls in the distance, reminding us of the danger lurking everywhere.

We draw back from each other at nearly the same instant, bumping against our seats.

Breath heavy—as loud as my heartbeat—I don't explain away anything. It wasn't the right moment, true enough. It was also the perfect moment, because this is the situation we met under—caught between traffickers and a serial killer. A situation where there might not be an easier or better tomorrow… a situation where there might not even *be* a tomorrow.

When our breathing evens out, I say, "Are you ready?"

He clears his throat and adjusts himself in his pants. "Born ready, luv."

Chapter 15
Dada

With my mind somehow put straight by that glorious kiss with Sean, I survey the flat desert expanse before getting out of the Cadillac. Thanks to stars being brighter than any I can remember seeing and a bright partial moon, it's fairly light out. I probably won't need the flashlight in my bag or the night vision goggles I've hooked around my neck. Grabbing my backpack, I open the door, which cracks with a metal *snap*, as I step out.

Sean, already outside, buttons up his flannel then walks to the trunk.

I meet him there, and he opens it, but he's disabled the trunk light.

I take out my flashlight after all, needing it to look inside.

A shovel, rope, highway flares, and toolbox line the dingy black fabric.

"What's your pleasure?" he says.

Dios. If I told him *that,* we'd never leave the car. "Shovel, rope, and flares for sure. What's in the toolbox?"

He opens it, and before I can tell him to grab the headlamp, he's pulling out the headlamp and slipping it over his head.

"I think that'll do," I say.

His adorable face furrows into uncertainty before clearing when he grabs a screwdriver. "It might not shoot far," he says holding the screwdriver aloft before shoving it into his back pocket, "but it'll cause some damage."

Picking up the shovel, he lays it across one shoulder, and

without any more agreement than the sound of the trunk slamming shut, we head across the desert.

I trip over some brush right away, skip-hoping to save myself a fall.

He flicks on his headlamp, guiding us, and we keep going, relying on his light and my cell's navigation.

Two hours later, we're at the coordinates, or so says the app Gracie developed for The Guild. That's one of the best things about The Guild—having access to cutting-edge technologies, both medical and mechanical.

Still, we could use a metal detector, because the markers here aren't helping our search. Except for the odd shrub and cactus and the faint odor of flowers, the desert hasn't changed much during our walk. There's nothing around us to suggest anything is here. I'm starting to worry we've wasted precious time in our search for Rosa.

Swallowing panic, I tell Sean, "Let's split up to search. I'll use my NVGs. Kick, tap, move even those things that look like they belong to the earth. If there's something here, it's well hidden."

"Got it," he says.

Though he hasn't complained once about his leg, I notice his gait has gotten worse during our walk, and he calls *me* determined.

We both get to work, pacing away from each other as we turn our desperate attention to finding something, anything. It's truly cold out here, cold enough that I lower my knit hat further over my ears.

"*Ach-y-fi.*" Sean steps on a bit of prickly bush with a cry. He bends down to rub his calf, grumbling, "Thing has daggers."

Repressing a grin that I'm a bit dismayed to find there, I ask, "You okay?"

"Fine. Watch the bushes."

I smile again. *Watch the bushes*? Hmmm… Dropping my bag, I reach in, grab protective gloves, quickly put them on, then begin pulling at the thorniest bushes around me. Ouch, even with gloves that hurts.

I continue pulling on those mean shrubs, feeling foolish but hopeful. Fate often puts obstacles in your path when you're close to getting what you want. Not because she wants you to lose, but because she needs to know you're serious.

After about the tenth bush, and having moved a good distance away, Sean calls over, "What're ya doin'?"

"Fighting fate," I say, grasping the top of a dead bush and pulling, despite it stabbing me in the wrist. There's a creak of steel hinges. The brush is attached to a steel lid that looks suspiciously like that found on an underground larder or root cellar. The mechanics are rudimentary.

"You're bloody brilliant," Sean says, making his way over.

Heart pounding, I hold up a finger to warn him as I pull the shrub-door the rest of the way.

It opens with a longer creak and a puff of air that smells like science class—formaldehyde. Hugging the inside of the dirt walls is an old wooden ladder.

Kneeling beside me, Sean says, "I'll go."

I shake my head. There's no way I'm letting him go down first, because he doesn't have a gun or my extensive training. He opens his mouth to argue, and I put a finger to my lips. That creak was likely loud enough to alert anyone down there to our presence, but no need to give information, like the number of people out here, to whoever might be hiding below.

Dropping my backpack, I remove and unravel a long, bendable cord. Inserting one end into my cell, I stretch out flat on the desert ground and feed the scope into the chamber.

An image of the inside of the underground chamber appears on my cell screen. A 360-sweep by the pipe camera reveals details of the five-by-five space tightly packed with boxes and a shelving unit with jars, but no humans.

Storage? With a flick of my fingers, I zoom in on the jars. Fermented foods? Clear liquid, maybe alcohol. What's that?

I zoom in on something behind the jars. Hmm, there's a metal a handle. It's a door. Oh. There's likely another chamber. Pulling the camera back out, I wind it around my cell, then slide the whole thing into my jacket.

Sitting up, I swing around, drop my legs over the mouth of the opening, and—

Sean grabs my arm. He shakes his head and mouths, *Let me go.*

I try to pull away, but he doesn't let go. *I'm not helpless,* I mouth back as agitation tightens my brow.

After a moment, with a curt nod, he lets go.

Heart rocking harder than a grunge band, I take out my Glock, flick on my NVGs, then drop.

My feet hit compact dirt with a thick thud that bends my knees. Lords and ladies, a firefight in an underground lair would prove a challenge.

I spin around, rechecking the area, then flick up the NVGs. They're not helping, because they require more ambient light to work properly. Raising my gun, I hit the light on the short scope, then run the beam along the ceiling. It's lined with wood rafters. This place is well built and cold enough to be a meat locker.

Swiveling back, I check the door behind the shelves. The handle and lock look new, so chances are high this place is still in use. Now to see what's behind the door. We're going to need to move the shelves.

Sean lowers himself down. His feet reach the ground while his hand is still on the top rung. And though I can stand in the space, which is just over six feet, he has to bend his six-foot-seven frame at the neck. He adjusts his headlamp and joins me by the door.

As soundlessly as possible, we visually inspected the containers. No trip wires. No sensors. The shelves have holes where each glass jar sits that are the exact size of the bottom of each one. I scan the legs of the shelving unit. It's on wheels.

Reassured that we can move it without breaking anything or

setting off a hidden alarm, I use my hands to demonstrate what we need to do.

Sean nods, but stops me when I try to help him move the shelves. He mouths, *I got it. Keep ready.*

I see the wisdom in his plan. He's obviously capable of moving it himself, and it's better for me to be prepared for whatever or whoever might be back there.

I step back, take a defensive stance, and ready my weapon.

Sean mouths, *One, two*, then swings the door open on *three*. The jars clank and the metal rattles, but the shelving system works as designed, so nothing falls or shatters.

Once he's cleared the door—my hands sweating in my gloves, heart pounding, mouth dry—I scan the door for any cameras or alarms. Again, there's nothing.

Obviously, no one expects company in a place in the middle of the desert, miles from humans, hidden under a shrub. No wonder Geraldo never found it.

Sean reaches for the handle, and I keep my weapon raised, but the door doesn't budge. Locked.

Dropping my backpack, I unzip a side pocket and take out my lock-picking kit. It takes me long enough that sweat beads on my forehead and my molars ache from grinding them before I hear the click. Finally done, I step back.

With a signal to Sean, I raise my gun again, providing him cover.

Gripping the handle, he yanks the door open.

A burst of rotting and rancid air rolls over us.

I gag. Though my eyes water, I keep them open and focused on the doorway, but no one comes out.

Nose buried in the crook of his elbow, Sean issues a low, angry growl.

Looks like I'm not the only one acquainted with the smell of death.

Behind the door is another tunnel that slopes dramatically, almost like a slide, preventing my light from showing what's down there. I wait a beat, listening for any noise or for anyone to come out.

Everything remains silent and unmoving, so I drop my weapon and pull out a tactical medical kit from my backpack. With a click, I open it and take out two heavy-duty, copper-lined filter masks that are better than nothing.

After we put them on, I signal to Sean that I'm going first. He squares his shoulders in a dramatic way that seems to indicate it's taking everything in him to let me take the lead. With that settled, I crouch-run down the ramp with the light on my scope leading the way.

Sean follows, forced to slide on his butt thanks to his size.

At the bottom, the tunnel expands into a tall, earthen chamber, braced with person-sized shelves, stacked with varying levels of decomposing corpses.

"Fuck." Sean throws his light along the bodies and frantically begins to scan. "Not here. Not here. Oh, Rosa, please don't be in here."

He's tall enough to see and reach the bodies on the highest shelves. His hand stretches out to one and then another body. He pushes hair from a face and gives a heartbreaking gasp muffled by his mask.

My heart drops. "Is it her?"

"No," he says, lowering his hand. "I don't know her."

Struck wordless in the middle of this nightmare, I nod and silently promise myself that the person responsible for this will pay. Even if that person isn't part of the mission I'm technically here for.

"Sean, we can't stay here long. That smell means death in more ways than one." Decaying bodies give off hydrogen sulfide, carbon dioxide, and methane. "The dead down here seem too far gone to be Rosa, but let's check quickly. When we're done, we can head back and make an anonymous call to the policia."

I don't add that I can't face off with the policia in this guise because I'm sure he gets it. At night, in the dark, on the street, it would be hard to associate me with Sister Dee, but that wouldn't hold up to any close scrutiny. If they suspected my cover had been compromised, The Guild would order me home quicker than they could say *serial killer*.

With a nod that seems all he can manage, we turn to begin examining the others.

Weary and ready to be out of here, I finally get to the last body on my side. There's something glinting on the corpse's chest. Cringing, I pull it out then realizing what it is, I shudder. "Sean. Look at this." I hold it up to him. "A weird place to find a nail file, right?"

He takes it from me, examines it under his light. "It's his."

"Who?"

"Armand. He's got a dozen of these things. Man's obsessed with his nails."

"It looks ordinary, though," even though there's dried blood, "with no special markings."

"It's his."

"It's not really proof, but along with the bodies, it might be enough to get Javier to do his job."

He grunts his agreement. "Let's get out of here."

We turn at nearly the same instant when an explosive noise stops us dead.

I shove Sean to the ground and dive next to him as the noise moves like thunder, down the tunnel and a heavy spasm of heat and pressure, dirt and grit, slams us.

Chapter 16

Sean

Something heavy drops across my back, pinning me. Face pressed into dirt, fighting for air, I cough and shift as creaks and groans settle around us like a closing coffin lid.

Ears ringing, leg barking fire, I fight the pressure against my back, shoving into a pushup to dislodge the heavy debris. It takes all my strength to throw off what I assume is wood from the shelving… but turns out to be bodies *and* wood from the shelving.

I near vomit. Air coated with dust rushes into my lungs. *Fuck.* "Dee?" I break into a fit of coughs. "Dee, you hurt?"

She emits a series of her own hacking coughs, but manages, "I'm fine." Her flashlight flicks on illuminating curtains of dust-soaked air and the fact that she's already on her feet. "You?"

Feels like someone took a hatchet to my leg. "Aye. Fine. What happened?"

Speaking delivers dirty air to my throat, and I break into another coughing fit. My mask is gone, so I spit, then tug my shirt collar up over my nose and mouth.

"A booby trap, likely." She sounds angry. "I missed it."

Her light flashes toward the tunnel we came down. There's a gap leading up, though debris clogs the entrance. It's open enough to climb up to the next chamber. It's impossible to tell what lies that way. That's where the explosion was. "Let's see if we can get out of here."

I inch my way to her, and she uses her light to guide me past fallen bodies, broken limbs, and debris.

"Hold your light there," I tell her, spotting my headlamp under a body. Apologizing to the dead, I tug it loose and find my mask wrapped up in the straps. Cuffing off the dirt, I slip on the mask and test the headlamp. It still works. I put it over my head.

Dee goes back to shining her light toward the narrow gap leading up. "The dirt covering the bodies should help with the escaping toxins," she says, coughing even though she has her mask on. Which makes me wonder how long the filters on these can last.

When we make our way to the slope leading up, she points her light at my leg. "You lied. You're hurt."

"One to talk," I say, guiding my headlamp over her head. "You're bleeding."

She puts a hand up to her forehead and almost to herself says, "I'm usually much luckier than this."

"Well, if it's any consolation, you're the luckiest woman down here."

She snorts at my dark humor. Together, we move out debris and rocks, crawling the slope to the upper chamber. My hands bite into stones as we work through the narrow passageway.

When I'd first slid down this part, it hadn't seemed near this long.

The nerve-rattling cracks, pops, and squeals give off a muffled quality. Makes every inch seem like we're working our way out of the gullet of a whale. Like we've been swallowed whole by the earth. Suppose we have.

"Sean." Dee rolls back a heavy rock with a shove.

I pick it up and throw it behind me. "Good thing we weren't in the front chamber," I say as we come to the end. The beams in the back held, saving us. Here?

Dee shines her light, and we stare at the sloped wall of dirt that blocks the exit.

I flash my own light along it. Debris. Jars. Glass. Beams.

The chamber has partially collapsed, but it's not as bad as it could've been. The heavy open door to the lower chamber caught and supported the shelf. Together the two hold up a great deal of the dirt and beams to our right. A tilted triangular ceiling. Best not to press on it.

I flash my light into dusty angles, trying to find a way out.

"There it is," she says, and I startle, swinging my head and my light where she points.

She's pointing at one of the beams from the ceiling. It's cracked in half, one end of it held up by the steel door. It has black residue along it. "What?"

"That's where the explosive was hidden. It must've been triggered by something down below. How did I miss it?"

"Ah, well, good to know," I say, with enough sarcasm that she snorts in answer. "Want to help me sort a way out of this now?"

"Already have," she says, directing her light into the area above where the blackened beam lies to a hole the size of a toddler's head.

I inch over in a low crouch. "Can you move over a touch, so I can get closer?"

She squeezes to the side, allowing me to examine it. The hole goes deep. I stick my arm up it. Can't reach the end, which means there's less dirt above us than I thought. "Actually, I think you *are* lucky."

"The luckiest woman down here," she says, repeating my bad joke, "but not lucky enough to have carried the shovel down."

I groan with the reminder as I grope around the hole. After a moment, I'm sure. "I can dig us out of here with the screwdriver in my pocket."

"We have until the chemicals from the decaying bodies kill us or we run out of air. Perhaps three hours."

No pressure. "Right, then. Let's get started."

"Careful, we need to buttress as we go," she says. "Right now, a lot of this is held up by that heavy door. Digging out could cause a collapse."

If it wasn't a heartbreak down here with a side salad of

despair, I might laugh at that. "When I was a child, my da, disreputable banker that he was, taught me to dig hidey-holes each time we moved."

"I take it you moved a lot."

"Let's just say, if there's one thing I know how to do, it's dig."

Chapter 17

Dada

I can no longer tell how long Sean and I have been in this dark underground chamber. My hands have gone numb except for the blisters on my palms which are sensitive and sore and soaking the inside of my gloves with pus.

Digging at an angle, I rest my head against the dirt tunnel that is now big enough for my shoulders and head. We still must be careful because we've only dug about a foot and half and still haven't found anything to indicate we're getting closer to air.

No. We've found something else entirely.

I scratch again at the steel material above me and recognize a portion of the lid that once hid this place.

Damn.

I don't give up easily, but I also don't ignore reality. We're running out of air. Sickness and exhaustion have set in. I try again to lift it, but it won't budge. No telling how much dirt lay beyond it. Which means we need to dig around it.

But which direction? If I dig the wrong way, dig in the direction that leads to more debris… we can't afford the time a mistake will cost us.

Panting, climbing down, fingers numb and somehow in pain, I exit into the wider chamber and drop down beside Sean into the dirt. We've been taking turns digging while the other stays still, so we'll use less air. Leaning back against the earthen wall of dirt, I hand him the headlamp.

He takes it with steady hands. "My turn?"

I shake my head, and a wave of dizziness washes down my body and turns my stomach so hard I fight not to retch. The air is thick, and our breathing is labored and heavy. We can't escape the fact that we're poisoning the air every time we exhale.

Pulling my flashlight from my pocket, I point it through the area we dug out. I can't say the words, but I hear his groan of understanding when he spots my light shining along the dirty metal above. He rubs at his forehead, leans his head against the wall of dirt behind him.

Unable to take a full breath or quell the rising panic, fear, and my pounding heart, I grope for and pull down my mask. "I don't understand. I've answered Fate's challenge every time. Even as a child, when I should've died."

I'm so mad, so disappointed in myself and so frustrated that I can't hold back the pain. A tear traces its way down my face. "I'm so sorry, Rosa."

Sean reaches over, wipes the tear. His hand cups my face. "Luv, don't cry."

Is there anything more likely to make a person cry than someone gently suggesting they *not* cry? I cover my eyes with my hands, desperate to hide my tears.

He pulls my hands away, kisses my cheek and the tears. Welcoming his touch—because it might be the last and only comfort we have to give each other—I lean forward and kiss him lightly on the lips.

He moves his mouth to my ear and whispers, "Would've liked a lifetime to get… to know… you."

Gooseflesh tingles down my body. There's nothing left but that immediate truth between us. The reality of this situation requires honesty. Escape is near impossible. There's too much debris, and chances are slim we'll find a way past that door. I kiss his sweat-and-dirt-stained lips. "I'm not a nun."

He laughs gently against my lips. "I know."

With that, our lips collide and greedily use up oxygen. Heart aching in my chest, all the passion of a not-likely lifetime thick in my chest, my breathing short, darkness begins to tinge my consciousness. I don't break the kiss. Sean does.

He grips my face in his hands and wipes my tears with his thumbs. "I'm not done fighting Fate."

His undefeatable spirit touches me. "You'll win," I say, hoping I'm not lying. "A lifetime awaits."

Taking the screwdriver, Sean shimmies into the dug-out area and I rest back against the dirt. The sound of his digging reaches me as I twist my leather bracelet and close my eyes.

Regretting the future now instead of the past, I drift off.

"Broke through."

I hear Sean's words as if from a distance, and I struggle to wake, struggle against a sleep as thick and heavy as a tomb.

I open my eyes, blink at his headlamp light. "How long have I been out?

"I broke through," he says again.

Is he for real? I can hardly comprehend this reprieve. Something hopeful rises in my chest. I'd resigned myself to dying down here. "Verdad?"

He nods. His smile is as bright and warm as the rush of understanding that lifts the fog of sleep and my heart. I lean forward and kiss him lightly on the lips. "You did it."

He smiles wider. "Go. You first."

Unable to muster enough strength to even wipe sweat from my eyes I slow crawl up into the hole, shimmying shoulders and elbows up, then bracing my feet against the sides so I don't slide back down.

Panting, I reach the end and find that Sean made the absolute right choice by choosing to dig to the right of the metal door. The area he dug out is nearly wide enough for us to escape. With a little more work, we can squeeze out.

I gulp in cool night air. I reach up and my hand slaps against a bar. It halves the opening. *Oh no*. Another obstacle, but this one won't stop me. I see instantly I could squeeze out. He's made enough room for me to get through, but his shoulders are easily twice the width of mine.

I'm too angry for sobs. I whisper-rage down at him, "You think I'm going to escape and leave you here?"

"Get out. Call the policia from a safe location. They can dig me out. Plenty of air now."

"No," I say, and squeeze my shoulders past the bar. It shifts. Not a bar. The shovel!

From despair to hope that quickly, I lower back down, wrap my hands around the handle, and begin to push and pull, push and pull to dislodge it.

Dirt sifts down over me, burning my eyes. I cough and turn me head, but I don't stop.

"Stop," Sean says. "You'll collapse it. Stop. Go call the police. Leave me."

I can't stomach the idea of leaving him down there. Fate has, once again, set me a challenge, and I want her to know I'm damn serious when it comes to Sean.

I keep working the shovel, feeling it move, knowing there isn't that much dirt, not enough to cause a problem now. "Help me," I tell him. "It's the shovel blocking us, and I'm nearly there."

The big man places his hands on either side of mine and we shove and pull, shove and pull. I feel it moving, feel that we will soon be free. He feels it, too.

Sean growls and heaves up, lifting me with his might as the shovel gives way.

Chapter 18
Sean

Driving down a dark and deserted road bumping toward Oaxaca in the safety of my Cadillac—never been so happy to see anything in my life—I can't help but feel something is not right between me and Dee. She won't look at me and hasn't said a word since we got into the car.

I'm not a fan of that brooding silence. In fact, I need to break it. "Once we're clear of the area, we can use your burner phone to make an anonymous call to the authorities."

She nods but doesn't answer me. After all that happened underground—the tears, the scorching-hot kiss, the truth that she isn't a nun, the vulnerability of the near-death experience—what's going on?

Rolling onto a paved road that lets me know we're getting closer to town, I whisper, "Is everything okay, luv?"

She laughs and wipes a tear glistening on her cheek. "I wanted to give up, had given up, and you saved me."

"We saved each other."

"No, Sean, that's not true. You *saved* me, and now I want to do the same for you. I can find Sofía, I can find Rosa, and I can find the information on Walid, and that means you don't need to put yourself in danger anymore."

Like hell. I glance over and take her in. We washed up a bit with the extra water we'd had, but dirt still coats her pants. There's a smear across her face. Yet she's so lovely, it hurts. Not only lovely in appearance, but lovely inside as well. She's trying to warn me off.

"Not going anywhere, whatever you're doing, I've got your back. Promise."

She grasps her leather bracelet, a habit I now realize is tied to stress and maybe…guilt? "Even if I won't tell you my real name or who I work for?"

Bugger. That hurts. Then again, she only knows my real name by coincidence. "Even then."

A troubled frown line appears on her forehead. "Even if what I do isn't legal?"

She's not *working for any government? Or she doesn't have permission to be in Mexico working?* "Aye, even then. We didn't meet on the beach in Cancun or at a local gym or through an online dating app. We're here in the middle of something awful so the rules are different."

Luck, lifesaving. Risks, deadlier. Feelings… accelerated.

When she doesn't respond, my hands flex against the wheel and I try for patience.

It doesn't work.

I swing over to the side of the deserted road, turn the car off, then twist in my seat. Even if you never tell me your real name or who you're working for, as long as I know that what you're doing will stop horrors like what we saw tonight, I'm in."

A look that is open and raw and filled with want crosses her face.

My body flushes with desire. Can't help it.

She licks her lips then her eyes drop to mine. "Is your seat all the way back?"

"Aye." Tall men problems. I wish it went back farther.

Without warning, she swings her leg across my middle and straddles me.

My eyes nearly pop out of my head—not the only thing popping up right now.

Reaching down, she yanks the recline lever. My head bumps against the leather.

Staring up at all that beauty, wanting her as much as I've

ever wanted any woman in my life, as hard as I've ever been, I'm completely lightning-struck—electrified and unable to move.

My body thrums. The temperature in the car seems to have risen to a thousand.

She leans down and kisses me with her lush and demanding full lips.

Blazing flames erupt through me so thick and hot I forget everything but the very real, deep and throbbing pleasure.

She grinds against my aching cock, and I grip her arse cheeks. I'm not sure if I'm trying to slow her down or speed her up—or just hang on for the ride.

Her tongue dives into my mouth as her kiss deepens. I welcome her with everything I have. Our tongues glide hungrily against each other. Our racing breaths quickly steam up the rocking car.

Despite what Dee says, I think there *might* be such a thing as destiny. This woman against me right now… feels like she's meant to be mine.

Chapter 19

Dada

I don't care even a little that I'm in a car, on the side of the road, in the middle of the night. Nothing matters but the feel of Sean's lips against mine, the hardness in his pants against my softness, and the absolute certainty that I am so very alive.

Tonight, I've survived death in its many forms. I came so close to it in that tomb that now, I want to live. I want to feel. I want Sean.

My head spins with excitement and from lack of air—in a good way this time. This kiss is more important than breathing right now. When his large hand moves from squeezing my butt to under my shirt, I realize everything needs to move faster.

Even though he knows I'm not a nun, I can feel his hesitation. He's spent too long holding back from me and that stops now.

Breaking free of the desire that has me glued to him, I plop back onto the other seat.

"Sorry," hc pants, as his hands arc pullcd from me body. "Too fast?"

"Not fast enough," I say, slipping my pants down my legs and kicking them off.

His hungry gaze follows the movement. His mouth hangs open. He swallows. "What?"

"I need for you to let me do everything, Sean. Okay?" I take off my underwear.

He nods. "Yes. Okay. Yes."

I pull my shirt over my head, then strip off my bra and turn my attention back to him. I nearly laugh. Sean is sitting there, unmoving. "Are you okay?"

"Not sure what's going on here." he says. "Don't want to make assumptions."

Oh, he is so delightful. In my line of work, I've found that the switch from false identity to real one can be jarring, even for those who know me best. Possibly, the easiest way to get past the identity in which he met me is to be wholly and forcefully myself. I can do that. "Gorgeous man, I want to have sex with you in this car. So, if you'd like to have sex with me in this car, I need you to take off your pants."

I laugh as he whips off his shirt, revealing all that muscle and beautiful tattoo. He is Fine with a capital F. He pulls down his pants and boxer briefs so quickly that when he plops his gorgeous naked butt back in the seat, the car rocks, and his cock stands at attention, hard and ready.

"Stupendous. Looks like I scared you stiff."

He snorts. "Scared is not what I'm feeling right now, luv. Desperate. Hot. Ready. Did I mention desperate?"

Glancing down at his erection, I realize none of that is a bad thing. "Eres tan hermoso." I stroke him, then bend down, and kiss the tip.

He moans and thrusts up his hips.

A gentle laugh releases from me, even though all I want is to dip down and taste the sleek length of this beautiful man. No time for that, not here, not now

I move my head and kiss the gunshot scars on his leg. "So, beautiful." I pump my hand along his hard length.

With a moan he closes his eyes, puts his hand over mine, which slows down my stroking. "*You* are the beautiful one."

I need him right now. "Do you have a condom?"

For a flash, his eyes pop open and a panicked look crosses his face before relief surfaces. "Yes. Thank the Almighty. Glove compartment."

Reaching over, I open the glove compartment, find a box of condoms, and take one out. I rip off the wrapper, then stroke the condom down to the base of him.

The moment it's done, he's reaching for me. "Luv, ride me."

No need to ask twice. Straddling him again, I grip him hard and throbbing in my hand. Positioning myself, I lower onto his cock with a pleasured moan.

Sean growls something in Welsh, then thrusts, pushing deeper.

Tightening my thighs around him, I join my mouth to his as I rise then drive down, rise then drive down.

He groans into my mouth, his beard scratching deliciously, his big hands clutching at my thighs. His tongue dives into my mouth, matching my stroke-for-stroke rhythm.

The frictions builds quickly, tight and electric and pulsing between my thighs.

Unable to match my pace in this tight space, Sean raises his hips with, "Yes. Luv. Fuck, that's good."

He's right. I abandon myself to the pleasure he's bringing me, increasing my rhythm.

He gasps. "Slow. Going to lose it."

But I can't slow. I'm so close, and he is so hard and smooth. He fills every part of me, every part that I have had locked down and closed off for so long. The delicious friction tightens my core, driving me on. "Please, don't ask me to slow."

He grunts, kisses me sweetly along my neck. "Go on. I'll keep't up… all day, then."

An exaggeration, I'm sure, but a hot enough promise that it sends the coil of energy and delicious pressure rising, rising so tight I begin to moan. The orgasm breaks through me with a force that has me throwing my head back and crying out, "Come with me. Come with me."

His wet lips suck the skin of my neck. His strong hands squeeze my butt, helping me keep my quick pace. I frantically ride him, my head pressed between the window and his mouth as tingles continue to work through my body.

I can hear his every ragged breathy moan, and the spike of pleasure as he comes with a fierce growl and a rush of heat that scorches me even through the condom.

It's his hands more than my strength that keep my body going, so when he lets go, I collapse onto him, sated and exhausted.

He kisses me ear, his breath hot and heavy, his beard pleasantly scratching against my cheek. I fight to catch my own breath.

His hands rub lovingly against my bottom, and it is so affectionate a touch that I focus on it with a piercing awareness because this is tenderness. And it's unexpected.

We are so close he doesn't have to move to whisper in my ear, "You've undone me, luv. You've completely undone me."

Chapter 20

Dada

The convent is quiet and dark in the early morning hours during prayers. Back in my nun habit, my head bandaged from the first aid kit in Sean's car—smelling none too clean—I open the door, then sneak inside. I close it as silently as possible.

"Sister Dee."

Ah! Spinning, I grab hold of Sister Angelica as a matter of reflex, nearly locking her in a headlock before I regain my composure. I let go. "I'm so sorry, Sister Angelica. I'm not used to being snuck up on."

"I didn't sneak." She briskly brushes down her tunic. "I was standing right here when you came inside. You didn't see me."

Well, that doesn't usually happen. A long night is no excuse for getting sloppy. "Sister, I'm sorry and I'm very sorry to be breaking the rules like this. I can assure you this was about Rosa. I—"

Waving aside my words, Sister Angelica turns on her heel and commands, "Follow me."

Coño. It looks like Sister Angelica has reached the limits on her patience. I suppose I can't blame her. A nun sneaking out at night, disappearing during the day, avoiding chores, prayers, and church might be more than she bargained for.

Padding along behind her, I follow her into her compact and well-stocked office—books and more books, a giant standing globe, cherry red desk, and several worn but comfy leather chairs.

Sister Angelica stops by her desk. "I can't have this, Sister Dee."

Perhaps it's the tiredness in me or the desperation or the fear for Rosa, but I instantly feel my stubborn nature rise. I'm not a nun. I'm here to do a job, protect women. "Sister Angelica, I appreciate your situation, but I'm undercover. Surely you knew when Momma asked you to allow me to come here, I'd be doing things that weren't very nun-like."

The older woman shakes her head and meets my eyes with something that looks very much like disappointment. "Don't assume. It's an annoying American trait."

I don't follow my instant and angry instinct to adjust her perception.

Sister Angelica's foot taps rapidly against the tiles. Realizing she's giving us both time to calm down, I take a deep breath and read the words stenciled on the wall behind her desk, the words of St. Catherine of Sienna, *In the end, nothing that ever caused one pain will exist.*

I hope that's true. I hope pain disappears from the soul, but that isn't the world in which I now live. Here. Pain begets more pain.

Finally, Sister Angelica pushes her black-rimmed glasses up her nose. "I was going to say, I can't have you running around trying to solve a puzzle when I may have part of the answer."

"You know something about the disappearances?"

She leans partly against her desk and partly against her cane. "Yes. There was a man who was accused of making his fiancée disappear: Geraldo Gonzalez."

"Not to be rude, Sister, but I already know."

Sister Angelica snaps her cane against the tile floor. I've heard less concussive gunshots. "Twenty years ago, Geraldo was left at the convent door with a note saying he'd been rescued from his," she reddens, "whore mother and needed a new home."

Whore? It could be coincidence, but Sean told me Armand used that exact same word in describing me. He also said the man is low enough that he'd put nothing past him, including being our killer. That, combined with the nail file… It's another place to look.

"Do you know who left him?"

"No. We searched for his mother, but she was never found. After a few weeks, we reached out to an older woman in town, Sylvia Gonzalez. She had money, owned apartments, and, at the time, was healthy and active. She took him in and gave him her name."

Lord and ladies, no one in this town is who they say they are. I'd seen it. Sylvia is a bit old to have a biological son Geraldo's age. Sensing where she is going with this speech, I hold my tongue.

She says, "I've thought of it much over the years, and I believe Geraldo's mother was the first who disappeared."

"You're saying this has gone on for decades?"

"Yes."

"And you've said nothing?"

She shakes her head in denial. "I've spoken up many times. I even brought my thoughts to a mayor years ago, but she, too, went missing. Now and again, I seek out those who might help, but to this day there has been little progress."

Good Lord. "Was Geraldo's fiancée the last woman taken?"

"I don't think so. I believe another woman, a refugee, was taken last year."

As depressing as that is, it also suggests the killer keeps the women for a while. Madre de Dios, Rosa is likely alive. "And the policia have never had any suspects?"

"They've never solved the crimes or found answers, but some have tried, including the mayor who went missing."

"Odd that the comandante didn't hesitate to blame Geraldo. Did he know this has been happening for years?"

"Yes."

Pobrecito Geraldo. A baby separated from his mother through some horror, maybe murder. And when he grew up, separated from another woman, his fiancée, who was also probably murdered.

Bad luck? Or had someone hated his mother enough to torture the man?

Chapter 21
Sean

Thanks to the turmoil surrounding life lately, my flat has seen cleaner days. There are canvases everywhere along with papers and dishes. Honestly, I've had enough of it. I wash another dish and put it in the rack by the sink. This place is getting a thorough cleaning.

Seems wrong to do ordinary things like light the candle on the counter and wash the dishes, but it's better to be busy. Tonight, we follow Armand. And if Dee is right, we find Rosa.

I rinse another dish and imagine it all working out. Rosa found. Sofía found. That last might take more time, but it seems more likely now than ever. Dee's passed on Sofía's description to whoever she's working with in the States, Sofía's most likely destination. Those people are helping in the search.

All they're asking of me in return is something I've wanted for months now—to take down the traffickers by going into their organization.

A knock on my flat door has me wiping my hand on a dish rag and moving to answer. After checking through the chain, I lift it off, then swing the door open. An older, unfamiliar bloke. He's wearing a hoodie, looking down, and has gray, curly hair sticking out. He's an overweight fellow. I tell him, "Wrong door, mate."

He lifts his head, and I get a good look at a man who's had a hard life. His gold eyes gleam in sunken and darkened hallows in need of a good night—or decade's—sleep. His mouth is downturned, melting into deep jowls. He says in a voice that doesn't match his visage in the slightest, "I think it's the right door."

I nearly drop dead on the spot. I pull her inside. I shut the door behind her and lock it. For a moment, I simply stare, trying to find where this man ends and Dee begins.

"That's bloody incredible," I tell her.

She begins to peel off her disguise, removing tape from under the wig, so that the mask loosens at the edges.

"Thanks." She wiggles her fingers under the mask chin and lifts face and hair as if it were a sweater. "Did you recognize any part of me at all?"

"None." Even watching as she disassembles the rest of herself, I'm stunned.

She shakes out of the mask, putting the eerily intact face and hair on a nearby easel. "Good, hopefully Armand won't give me a second glance when I put a tracker on him tonight."

"Can't imagine he will," I say, then look closer at the mask. The tape on the sides was actually some kind of invisible tightening agent, a clear, stretchy drawstring.

She pulls a cord inside her hoodie sleeve, and the body that had appeared bulky deflates with a low hiss. The disguise seems to melt off of her.

"How long did this take you?"

"Two hours." Bending to remove brown construction boots, she steps out of the getup, leaving behind the shell of a man that droops into a four-foot-tall pile. She's dressed all in skintight black pants and shirt. She grins. "Which is to say, you're not getting rid of me until it's time for me to track Armand."

Who needs dishes to keep busy? I drag her to me. "That'll work."

I kiss her until my head spins, my cock aches, and she's moaning against me. I need—

I break off from her. "I want to paint you."

Her eyebrows go up. "Now?"

I can't help the smile that springs to my mouth when I hear

the tone of her voice, as if I'd suggested sacrificing a virgin on Easter.

"Aye. Now." I point at her clothes. "Take this off."

I expect her to object. I expect her to roll her eyes. I expect… not sure what I expect, but when she shrugs and tosses off her shirt, I begin to think I'm a total numpty. *Couldn't waited until* after, *mate?*

Playing it cool despite the sweat now dripping down my back, I watch as she strips out of her pants as well. It's like watching perfection offer herself to your eyes and the skills of your hands. My hands have the skills to do right by her, but my focus keeps shifting to where I'd like those hands to be. I've never been so hard in my life.

Clearing my throat, I say, "Uh, the couch'll work."

She gives the couch a dubious look. Can't rightly blame her. I rush around to my footlocker, grab a clean white top sheet, then drape it over the couch.

With a that's-more-like-it nod of her head, she positions herself on it. All that lushness. All that boldness. And not an ounce of inhibition.

"You are so perfect, luv," I say, moving to get my palette. Feels like I'm fighting to walk with a pole stuck down the front of my pants. I'm sure she notices. She's trained to notice things.

I begin to mix the colors on my palette, setting up before the easel and the blank paper.

"Now you," she says.

I lean out from the easel, get another glimpse of her, and fight not to join her on the couch. "Now me?" I repeat, because I'm starting to lose the ability to think straight.

She runs her hand along the smooth dark skin of her outer thigh. "Yes. Now you take off your clothes."

My eyes are glued to the movement of her hand, so that the words she's spoken are held at bay for a moment. They finally sink in.

I grin at her. "That'll be a first for me. It's usually the model who's nude."

"Mmmm," she says. "But I think this model requires a different form of payment."

I groan, stand, then begin to unzip. The sharp pain of my cock straining against my jeans heightens my every movement. I strip down, and she makes a pleased sound.

"You are glorious. You know that, right?"

"Ach. Stop, luv. I can't do this. Not with your eyes devouring me like that."

She laughs. "Too late. You promised to paint me. I'm not allowing you over here to devour *me* until it's done."

My eyes must surely pop from my skull, because she laughs hard enough to snort once.

"Not funny," I grumble. What started out as a fun—let me get a few strokes of all that beauty on a canvas—has turned into a test of my patience and skill.

She moans on the couch, arches, then groans. "How's this?"

Ach. She thinks I'm made of stone. "You mean to torture me, then?"

"Oh, I'm not the one who kissed me senseless then suggested I let myself be painted for two hours."

Two hours? Nope. I mix my paints, put brush to page, add some lines, then turn the canvas around. "Done," I say.

She bursts out laughing. "Sean!" She begins to laugh harder. "That's the best stick figure I've ever seen."

This last she laughs into my mouth, as I've crossed the room to her. I sweep my tongue into her mouth and revel in the skin-to-skin contact of all of her against all of me.

"Oh, luv," I say, pushing my aching hard-on against the smooth mound between her legs. I'm likely to come if I don't get control."

"I need you inside me," she says.

Ach. That's not helping. I pull back. "You're going to make me come."

"Yes, I am. But first put on a condom."

I'm a spry bastard when I need to be. I jump off the couch,

retrieve my britches from the floor, and fish out a condom. Ripping it open with my teeth, I lower back to the couch.

She takes the open package from me.

With a smooth tug of her hands, I'm wearing the protection. So turned on, I nearly come from that. No lie. I do some mental gymnastics, pulling my mind away from the sheer bliss of her body, all the lush skin, long enough that I regain control.

"Quickly," she whispers, writhing under me.

Control be damned. I push into her, swift and deep.

She groans and arches.

I moan with the feel of her slick wet heat gripping me.

She begins to move. "Please, Sean. Fast. Hard."

I've got to take a moment, adjust my hand against the side of the couch, but that change allows me, even with my bad leg, to thrust fast and hard enough to make the couch jump against the floor.

With every push, she makes noises under me that nearly do me in. A high-pitched, "Ay, ay, ay," that matches my deep, pounding rhythm.

I close my mouth around her cries, eating them, savoring them. I slip my tongue into her mouth and angle every thrust to meet her exactly where her body tell me she needs me to be.

"That's it," she says.

Like I don't already know. Like I can't already feel her reaction to me. The breathy, panting way she is losing herself to me.

We meet each other, stroke for stroke. Her breathing and moans accelerate until she is begging me, "Don't stop. Don't."

I've no bloody intention of stopping. Electric heat rides my body, tightens my abs, drives my hips.

With a high cry that is surely as close to Heaven as I will ever see, she comes around my cock.

I lose all rhythm to the frantic, desperate energy building so tight and strong in my balls and cock that I swear every inch of hair on my body rises. "Oh, luv. Luv." I bury my words against her neck as I drive into her again and again.

I can't hold back. Two more deep thrusts and I'm blinded by the pleasure. I come so hard I see stars. I groan and push into her warmth until I'm utterly spent and praising her with every word of gratitude I can recall in Welsh.

My body gives out nearly as hard as I came. I collapse on top of her, realize I'm crushing her, and roll off. I slam onto the floor.

Daft prick.

With a startled sound, she looks down at me. A smile on her lips, she shrugs, and rolls on top of me.

I catch her, nibble her ear, hold her to my chest as she laughs softly.

Aye. This is Heaven.

Chapter 22

Dada

An hour after I've arrived, I'm pleasantly nude, curled up with Sean on his bed, my legs intertwined with his, my head on his chest, listening to his rapid heartbeat slow back to normal.

Sweat and sex and candle wax coat the air. Thanks to the setting sun and the blinds he now ritually keeps closed, it's grown dark in the room.

His voice rumbles in his chest when he speaks. "You said something," he breathes out and I feel uncertainty in that pause. "Luv, when we were trapped underground. You said you were supposed to die as a child. Can you… would you tell me?"

My turn to let out a breath. That's not an easy story to tell. That story is rooted in my past. The silence stretches out. I wrestle with my demons, and he draws me closer to his side, squeezing me tight.

Suddenly, I find I not only want to, but I *need* to tell.

I know from my big family that developing a relationship as a person rescued from adverse circumstances gets complicated. It's a risk in many ways, but I feel I know Sean. He won't ever see me as only my wounds. That's the wonder of who he is. I breathe him in, the pleasing musk of his maleness, and relax into his strong arms.

In a voice so small it somehow seems to belong to the child I once was, I quietly say, "I was kidnapped from Puerto Rico when I was nine, taken by boat to New York City, and held captive in an apartment for three-and-a-half years."

The temperature in the room seems to change as Sean tenses beside me.

I look up to see his face a mask of both pain and anger. I know those feelings.

I kiss his chest. "I'm here. I'm safe. It's okay now."

He nods and chokes out, "I'm sorry, luv. So very sorry."

He kisses my head, the side of my face. He runs a hand down my arm. I hear his heart beating loud and unsteady. He whispers, "We're both survivors, it seems."

Oh, I do like this man. How easily he sees me not as what I endured, but how I've thrived.

"How did you get free?"

I pause for a moment, going back in time to that room, that apartment.

He doesn't rush me, waits for me to find my way forward as he strokes my arm and kisses me lightly again and again.

After a moment more I say, "When I first came to be held prisoner, I was conditioned to want and long for… the man who took me. I wasn't allowed out of my room. I rarely saw anyone else. I was given food and, because he knew I could read and that I craved learning, he brought me many books. I feared displeasing him and losing those small kindnesses. Years passed that way. Then I got pregnant."

Sean's breath rushes past my ear. He tenses, but stays quiet.

"After that, the man—whose name I no longer say because I have released him along with my pain—stopped coming into my room. He fed me sporadically. I believe he was trying to solve the problem of my pregnancy by starving me."

"Sinister fuck."

"Yes. Until that time, I hadn't sought to escape or rescue myself. It'd never crossed my mind to try. The absolute belief that I was his, the belief he'd programmed me with, was that strong. But when I had the child inside me and we were starving, I realized I had to find a way out."

I shake my head. "As if it were that simple. I cannot tell you how afraid I was of even the thought of defying him. I believed going against him was wrong in every way. I believed he controlled my fate, so to go against that… it didn't seem possible for myself. But for another, for the child, I did it. Trembling, terrified, I began to drop notes from the bathroom window of my prison."

"No one saw them," he says flatly, guessing the result.

"Someone did, actually. A boy. He came into the alley every day, picked up my notes, then ran off. I thought he'd bring me food. Help. What I didn't know, what I learned later, was that he kept them, saved them at home. He thought they were a game."

"Good Lord."

"When I went into early labor, the man I lived with came into the room, gagged my mouth, and left me. He never came back. I would've died. My body couldn't do what it was being asked to do. The boy who got my letters came, as he did now every day—when he saw there was no letter, he began to worry that maybe the letters were real. In a panic, he went to a police officer on the street, told him where he'd found the notes, showed him the letters.

"By luck or fate, something in the story motivated the officer to act. Not in a year. Not at the end of the week. Not even after contacting his department.

"He ran down blocks to where my letters told him I was imprisoned. He got the super to unlock the apartment and found me bleeding to death on the floor.

"Dear God."

"Yes. And on that same day, a day when I should've died, a day when my son *did* die, I was taken to the hospital."

"Oh, luv." Sean's voice is ragged, choked with tears. "A bloody miracle you survived."

I laugh gently, even as the tears roll from my own eyes onto his chest. "That is not the most miraculous part. What happened next delivered me from Hell to Heaven."

He squeezes me, whispers, "Tell me that because I need to hear the part where you are safe and loved."

A knot rises in my throat. To tell this part of the story—my rescue and my adoption—is to reveal enough that, if he knows about Mukta Parish, he can put it together.

Though I want to tell him, I'm conflicted. My loyalty is to my family, and it always will be. How can I turn from that simply because this man makes me feel less alone? More than that, he makes me feel… seen.

Even as I open my mouth, I'm not sure what I will do.

Chapter 23

Sean

Lying with Dee on my bed, I squeeze her tight and drink in the feel of her smooth skin, the scent of her body—rose and earth—and remind myself again and again that she's safe. But as many times as I repeat this to myself, I cannot let her go. Thankfully, she puts up with my strong embrace.

I kiss away her tears, grateful for her in a way that makes me a fan of God or angels or whomever gave her the strength to write those letters. Seeing her about to speak, I wait and tell myself that, if she stops now, I won't press.

She says, "Later that week, the police officer who'd rescued me was working overtime as security for a visiting dignitary, a wealthy woman who championed women's rights. He told her how he'd saved a girl held prisoner for four years.

"He told her how, after I'd given them my name, he'd learned I was orphaned—my papi, my only family, God rest his gentle soul, had died a year before.

"The woman was curious about me so, instead of going to the gala where she was scheduled to speak, she insisted he take her to the hospital to meet me."

"That woman adopted you?"

"Yes. Momma told me that, when she arrived at the hospital and saw me, gaunt and haunted, it was love at first sight."

Pulling back from her, I run my fingers along her cheek. Her honey eyes shine with tears. My heart feels as if it might break. "Can't blame her."

She draws in a breath, and I know I've rushed ahead, tiptoed into an area that feels right, but is not yet firmed by years of us knowing each other and making that connection.

Wanting to express the words without words, I kiss her. My tongue plays with hers, my lips possess and cherish her with everything I have.

She moans and arches into me.

The feel of her against me, her warm mouth, sends my head spinning and my heart sprinting. She is my miracle.

I cup the side of her face and give myself a moment to catch my breath before saying, "What was it like, walking into a new life?"

She laughs softly, breathlessly. "Strange and thrilling. Scary and magical. Overwhelming and transforming. I went from being alone all the time to being surrounded by people, their open hearts gentle and waiting, ready to hear me. I went from the poorest, most base of situations to being adopted by one of the wealthiest women in the world. Also, one of the most caring women."

Her eyes seem to be looking past me, past this room, directly into her past. "When I arrived, I'd been desperate for any reassurance that I mattered, and Momma gave that to me. If I walked into her office, no matter what she was doing or what world leader she was speaking to, she stopped for me, her face would light up, and she'd welcome me with open arms."

A tear winds its way down her cheek. "I used to go to her office to check, nearly every day. My therapist encouraged it, and Momma delighted in it, so I quickly learned I *did* matter. Not only to Momma, but to all of my adopted siblings—children rescued, like me, from tragic situations."

I'd press her for a name, but I don't need to. I'm not well-versed on much American high society, but I've heard of the Parish family. Heard of Mukta Parish, a woman who champions women's issues, a woman who adopts children all over the world from difficult backgrounds. I've heard of her, aye, but have never given her a second thought. Now, with Dee here, I wonder at this woman who saves hearts, and I pray Sofía one day knows that kind of healing. "How did you get involved in the work you do?"

She frowns and I realize this is where the sharing ends. I tell her, "You don't need to say."

She shakes her head. "You're asking me for the same reason I visited Momma's office. You want proof that you matter, and me sharing myself with you is that proof."

My mouth opens to deny it, but I realize she's right. I wait with a hard knot in my throat.

She shifts, bringing her eyes from looking past me to looking *at* me. She stares into my eyes, and I see her hesitation and nearly rush to tell her it's okay. But I can't. Not after what she said.

She places her hand against my jaw, runs a thumb along my beard. "At twelve, I flew to a home where I was surrounded by love and understanding. A home where I longed only for one thing—to help free others from situations similar to the one I'd endured; and this, too, Momma gave me."

"Ah," I say, freezing as the dominoes all line up. She operates outside the law. "You work for your mum, Mukta Parish. Is that who pays for you to investigate these things?"

She stills against me. Should I have pretended ignorance? Nah. Not how I want us to go from here. This was hard for her, revealing herself. She did it so that I'd know I matter. I want her to know I return the sentiment. "You're part of a wealthy family that does covert operations, a vigilante network. Your secret is now mine—to my grave. I swear it."

She grins as if she never had a doubt. "We prefer the term spies."

Cheeky. "And your family has been doing this for years?"

"That I can't answer."

"Okay. Don't take offense, but I thought you were government."

"Highly offensive."

Very cheeky. "Be honest with me; how likely is it that you and your family can help me find Sofía? Help us locate Rosa?"

"If anyone can find Sofía, it's them. But they don't know I'm searching for Rosa and would likely call me home if they knew how deeply involved with the search for a serial killer I am. Tonight, we're on our own when I tag Armand."

My skin crawls with the idea. He desires her; I saw it in his greasy eyes. "Luv, it's so dangerous. Let me put the device on Armand."

She shakes her head with determination. "No. Stop worrying. I was two inches from you and you didn't know it was me. Trust me. All I have to do is plant the tracker and back off. If he has Rosa, if he goes to where he's keeping her tonight, we'll find her."

"I trust you—as you trust me to be your backup."

A trilling sound comes from her phone. She jumps out of my arms and out of bed. I watch as she scrambles around the room picking up clothes.

"What're you about?" I say, tension rising in my shoulders.

"Didn't you hear my cell?"

"A text?"

She finishes putting on her shirt. "No. A summons." She grabs her phone, looks around the room, finds the one area with a blank wall, and sits herself in the corner. She looks up at me with serious warning in her eyes. "Not a word. They can't know I'm here."

They? Fuck. She means her family.

Chapter 24

Dada

Because Sean has exactly one area in his entire apartment without artwork on it, I'm sitting on his floor, squeezed into a corner, taking the call from my handler, AKA Tony.

Holding up my phone, I log into the secure site for the video call.

Tony's already there. "Hey, D," he says with a half-yawn, rubbing his hazel eyes.

I'm grateful his nickname for me matches my cover name. Actually, his nickname for all members of our team, except Bridget, for obvious reasons, is the first letter of our first names. He calls Bridget *Bridge*.

For someone who can figure out the most complex of cases, Tony likes to keep things simple. Today, that's a help since I haven't told Sean my real name.

Purposefully keeping my eyes on my cell and not on Sean, who has gotten out of bed and is quietly dressing, I say, "Past your bedtime? It's 9:30 PM."

"Forget what it's like here? I'm up early, teaching lessons. Including yours."

"Boohoo, I have to wake up in a mansion where people make me breakfast and clean my room," I say, holding my cell with one hand braced on my knee and wiping fake tears with the other. "Want to switch?"

In response, he laughs. "I don't like hats."

Funny. "What's this about?"

He shrugs. “Gracie’s call.”

Before I can question that, there’s another beep and Gracie pops on with a, “These are screenshots from Armand’s cell phone.”

Our boxes are moved to the side as a document takes the center of the screen. My sister is amazing when it comes to cyber intelligence.

I learn forward and expand the shot to get a look at the time stamp. “Are these…”

“Up to date,” Gracie says. “Some are minutes old. I was able to use the memory cache to hack into Armand’s cell, but have only been able to piece together a few. From what I’ve seen, Armand has a problem.”

“What kind of problem?” Tony asks, stepping on the exact question I almost got a chance to utter. Another rule of big families: speak fast.

Gracie twirls a Jolly Rancher in her mouth, presses some buttons, and scrolls texts until she comes to a specific one. She brings it up. “Walid had some missing *merchandise*. Armand says he’s found it and is bringing it to him tonight.”

Walid is very careful when discussing his business. He calls humans by hair-raising euphemisms like *product* and *merchandise*. I don’t look at Sean, but I have no doubt he can figure out what it means.

Tony asks, “How does someone go missing? Escape?”

“That’s where I started,” Gracie says. “But after a deep dive, I found these.” She clicks some more keys and emails pop up. “From what I’ve been able to put together, Armand is stealing women from Walid and using them for his own side business.”

“What kind of side business?” I ask, heart starting to pound.

“Femicide. He’s selling the experience, sex and murder. He’s got a very select clientele—an exact list will take time to uncover. It may be impossible, because a lot of the particulars take place on the dark web.”

There’s a long moment of silence. My brain readjusts from serial killer to… I begin to panic. I need to get into position at the bar. I need to follow Armand on foot. I need to find Rosa. Tonight. There's too many unknowns, too many dangers, too many ways Rosa could be disappeared.

"He's doing this on his own?" Tony asks.

Gracie shakes her head. "Seems like he might be communicating with another person, or maybe two. He never sends messages to the same number. He's very cautious."

My skin goes cold, and I sense Sean go incredibly still.

Tony asks, "D, didn't you mention women being taken from town during our last call? You got anything on this?"

I feel his question everywhere—in my panicking mind, in my tensed hands, in my aching heart. I need to get out of here. I need to answer. I need Sean to stop staring at me with those beautiful eyes, wide and shocked.

"Are you trying to bite your lip in half?" Gracie pipes up.

I unclench my teeth from my lower lip. Exhaling a tremulous breath, I say, "I'd thought Armand was a serial killer. I wanted to find more information…"

Tony grunts, a noise that lets me know he doesn't like where this is going.

But… what's done is done. "I… I found a tomb with at least thirty women buried."

Tony shifts forward. "Found?"

Gracie asks, "Did the bodies show the same cause of death, similar wounds like with a serial killer?"

My stomach pitches. I'm half-talking with them and half-mentally calculating the time I need tonight. Armand typically arrives at the bar around eight and leaves around midnight. If I finish here quickly, I'll still have enough time to get into my disguise and follow him.

I try to pull out the worry that has my heart focused on Rosa so that I can answer. "I wasn't able to ascertain causes of death, but from what I could see…" Gracie's new information clarifies what I'd noticed in the tomb and would likely have put together before now, if not for the explosion. "No. They were different."

"Fucking awful," Tony says. "Sorry, this is happening around you, D. You okay?"

"Wait," Gracie says. "Armand is stealing from Walid. What would Walid do if he found proof of that theft? Say, a tomb where thirty women were buried?"

Tony's eyebrows rise. "If we have Sean alert Walid to what's going on, Walid can take that fucker Armand out and stop the killings. Bonus: it gets our asset, Sean, in good standing with Walid, leaving us an opportunity to place an operative deep into his organization."

I don't panic. Well, *normally*, I don't panic. Maybe that's why it's so hard to control this need to get out of here now. Time is ticking away. I feel it. I need to act tonight.

"That plan will take too long," I say. "A woman's life is in danger. She has a child. I'd like team approval to act tonight. To follow Armand and take him out if necessary."

"Thousands of women's lives are in danger," Tony says, frowning. "I know it sucks, but taking out Walid's head of security isn't recon. It's straight-out attack. We don't want to alert these guys we're on to them before the actual attack. It could ruin years of planning."

"Don't be insensitive," Gracie says. "Whose life? Do you need us? Tony and I can fly out ASAP. We'll be there in the morning."

"No!" I blurt, "That's not fast enough." Maybe if they think my life is in danger, they'll see I need to act now. "Armand has it in for me. Going after him is a matter of *my* safety."

"You've been keeping this from me?" Tony says, sounding hurt and offended. "I've been blessed with some nut-job sisters. I'm pulling you."

"No, you're not," I object. Both Tony and Gracie stare at me. I know. I know. It's Tony's call as my handler, but I don't care.

I *can't* care.

"Dada," Tony says, "Where are you?"

Coño. "I've got to go." I reach for the phone.

"Dada!"

I close the browser. My cell buzzes instantly, but I ignore it and run a hand along my wrist. Not along my bracelet, but along the GPS embedded under my skin. There is one under the skin of every member of The Guild.

If they need to, my family will be able to find me. Or my body.

Sean clears his throat.

I look up.

He says, "Guess it's me and you, Dada."

Chapter 25

Dada

The bar doors are thrown open to the warm night air. Patrons with drinks in hand, stand inside and out. Smoke and Daddy Yankee pour onto the dimly lit Oaxaca streets, but the music is secondary to the game on three different screens: Club América versus Cruz Azul.

Despite the festive atmosphere, I'm practically fidgeting on my barstool. My eyes are glued to a screen, but my focus is to the right of the screen on the door leading from Armand's upper-level room.

I'm still a basket of regret after that call with Tony and Gracie. Maybe I should've tried to convince them more. If I had Gracie working with me, she'd be able to track Armand's cell and tell me if he's here. As it is, I'm tearing bits of napkin under the whiskey glass I'm nursing, waiting to see if Armand follows his regular routine and comes out around midnight. If he's not here? I honestly don't know what I'll do.

I dislike going against my family like this, and I can't help but wonder what they're up to since my cell stopped buzzing. Reassuring, actually. It means they've accepted that I'm doing this and shouldn't be bothered with useless calls.

It also means Tony is likely on a plane right now.

I'll deal with him when he gets here.

"You okay, luv?" Sean's voice, like a balm to my nerves, filters through my earpiece.

I bring up my drink to hide my response. "Yes," I mumble into my glass.

"As you suggested, Geraldo is on his way over to meet me. He knows how to use the gun you left in the glove compartment, fights like a madman, and wants to end this for his fiancée. We'll be your backup."

"Good," I say into my glass, taking a sip then putting it down.

I'm grateful that Sean finally agreed to my demand that he invite Geraldo to partner with him. Going after one serial killer is a lot different than going up against two or more men engaged in selling femicide.

I'd put Sean into a ring against anyone, but having someone who's willing to shoot a gun is necessary. Plus, I'm glad to offer Geraldo a chance to take down the man who killed his fiancée.

The plan is that Sean and Geraldo will follow the tracker I put on Armand, and I'll follow Armand. Sean wanted to wait outside the bar and follow along with me, but I explained that it might make him feel better, but Armand would surely spot two people following him versus only me. Instead, he is waiting a few blocks away and will track Armand by following him without ever entering onto the same street Armand and I walk. This way, we can meet up at the final destination, and if Javier or whoever else Armand is working with shows up, we'll have enough people to control the situation. I hope.

Despite what I told Sean about my disguise, I'm nervous about bumping into Armand. I have to *literally* bump into him in order to press the tracker onto him, and I have to do it while managing a weight I'm unaccustomed to. Sure, the bulk of my disguise is compressed air, but the suit still weighs a ton.

Those added pounds gives me the appearance of being a big guy moving my weight around. People can notice, sense something is off, if they see a large person moving with the lightness of someone half his weight. It's like watching an actor in a movie carry a suitcase that obviously has nothing in it. The eye unknowingly picks up on the detail, diminishing the illusion.

Of course, in a movie the only thing risked is the suspension of disbelief. For me, if Armand looks too closely, I'm risking Sean's life, Geraldo's life, Rosa's… and mine.

The door by the bar opens and Armand exists. Gracias de Dios.

Heart pounding, breath unsteady, I stretch as he passes, bumping him with my arm. I turn and pat his shoulder in apology, securing the tracking device.

Armand curses and shoves me off. For all intents and purposes, I appear to be a heavyset older man with gray hair, large nose, and stooped shoulders. His eyes sweep over me and then away, as if he has bigger fish to fry.

My stomach heaves. That man… there was something vile in his eyes, something vicious. That was a man intent on murder. It's all I can do to repress a full-body shudder. I have no idea what happened upstairs in his office, but for some reason Armand is filled with fury.

I shift the weight of the padding, drop from the stool, then follow Armand out onto the dark streets. The extra weight is cumbersome enough to make my exit labored. Was this disguise a mistake? No. That's nerves talking. It was chosen for all the right reasons and the weight isn't so heavy that I can't adjust.

Outside, it starts to drizzle, warm and wet. Ahead of me, cursing under his breath, Armand lights a cigarette. The sour smoke hits my nostrils. Not a cigarette. Something stronger to soothe his frazzled nerves. All the better.

Keeping track of him for many blocks, I drop back when he stops and pivots. My pulse pounds. My hands sweat. Did he see me?

Likely not. I'm far enough away that I can only see *him* through the reflection of a glass window across the street.

I keep my gaze on the sidewalk as Armand doubles back and heads through an alley. He's practicing a surveillance detection technique, which means he has a reason to not want to be followed. He's leading me to her; I can feel it.

After a moment, I move to the corner and follow. I catch up

as he slips into what appears to be an out-of-business corner grocery.

The windows are painted black—the universal sign for not wanting people to see inside. In this case, me. There's no way for me to see what me and my team are walking into, but I know enough. Armand is in there and likely Rosa. I pray there's no one else in there, like Javier, a man trained to use a gun.

Shrugging the extra weight that aches against my shoulders, I glide around to the back door. Dropping low, I squat beside a gray steel covered basement window and quietly take off my disguise.

I press my earpiece to contact Sean, get his ETA, when a soul-shattering scream penetrates through the window. I know that voice. It's followed by the sound of flesh hitting flesh.

I tap my earpiece, bark out, "Hurry, Sean. Rosa is here, in need. I'm going in."

Only static answers me, and I pray Sean received my message as another muffled scream reaches my ears. Because I've face situations like this before—I've done undercover work for over a decade—I also know that waiting isn't an option. Armand is not in control of himself. I saw it in his eyes tonight.

My heart in my throat, I pick the lock on the store's back door, take out my weapon, then enter. A squeak and scuttling movement make me jump back.

Coño. A rat scurries across a one-time storage room that's been turned into a makeshift kitchen. There's a folding table and some chairs, an electric griddle with grease congealing across it, a series of plastic containers with food and numerous discarded beer bottles.

Weapon raised, I slip through the storeroom into the grocery store. Rotten and blackened food in glass refrigerators line the back wall. I clear each aisle, making sure no one will come up behind me, before sliding past a rolling bucket with a mop sticking from the top and heading toward a door I know is the basement. I know, because Rosa issues another hair-raising scream before cursing and saying, "Don't touch me, you filthy dog!"

"How's this for a touch?"

There's a jarring slap.

"Or this?" Another thick slap.

Cold fury erupts in my body as I head down the stairs. I hear chains rattling. Pushing aside the anger that wants to make me sloppy and the fear that wants to make me turn and wait for backup, I keep moving. Calm and focused, every step measured and brought down with absolute quiet, I descend.

The stairs are dark, enclosed by brick, but light streams from around the corner. On the last step, I take a calming breath and send a prayer that my abilities are enough, that my training, what I've prepared for my whole life since being rescued will hold true. It's not my first rescue mission, not by a long shot, but it feels so very personal.

I pivot around the corner. The basement is unfinished cinderblock, ancient and moldy.

Armand is turncd from mc. I aim at his back, prepare to shoot as he is still trying to unchain Rosa, but it's not a clear shot, because Rosa is fighting back, jerking her body this way and that making it difficult. I can't risk hitting hcr.

Suddenly, Armand heaves around and faces me.

The first thing I notice is the gun in his hand, the gun resting against Rosa's head, and then, I see Rosa's sunken and tearful eyes. Her face shows signs of bruising. Her lip is busted. My stomach flips. Sour bile rises into my mouth. I keep my gun trained on Armand.

Armand smiles, a smile as cold and confident as any I've ever seen. "And here is my other whore."

Chapter 26

Sean

Sitting in my car, blocks from the bar, I grip my phone, willing it to deliver the information. Something must've gone wrong. The tracker Dee was supposed to put on Armand should've sent the guy's location to this phone when he left the bar, but the screen is blank.

"It's not working," I tell Geraldo.

He looks at me nervously, tilts the phone in my hand, so he can see it. "Dead?"

I cringe at his word choice. "No. It's got a charge, mate, and this all worked fine earlier."

I hit my steering wheel. "Bollocks. It's been forty minutes."

I've texted Dee three times. No response. Trying not to panic, I punch her number into my phone. It doesn't go through, and we tested the call before she left too. What changed?

Geraldo looks out the window and down the street, as if he's planning to start walking around, looking for her.

Bugger. I got one last option. "One sec," I tell Geraldo.

I reach into my cup holder, pull out the burner phone Dee gave me for emergency use only, and step out of the car. I walk down the street so Geraldo can't hear.

Dee, Dada—that's a lovely name—would not want him to know any of this. And I'm sworn to secrecy.

I open the phone and hit the one number she'd programmed into it.

A man answers. "D?"

"Hi, Tony, mate, this is Sean—" Fuck. Should've said Juan. "Dee's informant. I need your help."

I hear static and noises I can't place. He says, "What's going on?"

"She's trailing Armand. I'm her backup. I'm supposed to give her a hand," I don't mention Geraldo, who has gotten out of the car and is now watching me. He wants her safe as much as I do, and to finally prove his innocence. "Problem is, the tracker she put on him, the one that's supposed to follow him isn't showing up on my phone."

"Hold," Tony says, "checking her GPS."

GPS? What does that mean? I press the phone hard to my ear, trying to hear into the room where Tony has the cell muffled.

I hear him shout, "Fuck protocols! Give me the information." A split second later, he's back. "Sean?"

"Here."

"Last known location is a street corner. It's not exact, but, chances are, when you get eyes down there, the place you're looking for will be obvious. Look for a place that practically begs you to stay away. Her last known is two miles from where you are now."

How does he know where I am? "Last known?"

"It's the last place her signal came through. After that, her signal winks out. My guess is she went into a building with advanced jamming equipment. I've sent the nearest street corner, because jammers, whether handheld or bigger—have a limited range. In this case, it's probably one or two buildings, so she'll be close to her last known."

The phone in my hand beeps. I look, expecting to have to locate the text message on this unfamiliar phone, but what appears is a map with a blinking red dot. I'm that dot. How the fuck?

Back by the car, Geraldo is pacing.

"Thanks, Tony," I say, as I motion Geraldo that it's time to go. He slips into the passenger seat.

Tony asks, "Do you have a gun?"

Ice-cold dread snakes through my body. "Aye. Dee left one in the glove compartment."

"You don't sound super confident."

"Never shot a gun before."

A pause. "What kind of weapon? I can walk you—"

"No, mate. She's given me instructions before, and you're not going to make me an expert in"—I look at my phone—"eight minutes." I don't tell him I have someone here who *can* shoot because I'm sure that would only bring about more questions. I tell him, "I've got to…" I swallow a ball of panic, "get her."

"Call when you have her safe."

Makes it sound inevitable. "Will do."

I hang up. Heart pounding, teeth grinding, I run down the street to the car.

Haven't run full-out since my injury. Box like a madman, lift weights, cross-train, but run? Hurts my soul as much as my leg. Hadn't been sure those muscles would still work.

Luckily, they do.

Not even winded, I swing back into the car, hand Geraldo the cell with the info, then turn on the car, pull out, and explain, "The cell has Dee's location. Give me directions as they appear."

"Got it," he says, and proceeds to snap and point as a way to give me step-by-step directions. A few blocks later, he says, "She's there!" He points at an abandoned grocery store.

I pull over. Throat bone dry, I reach past him, open the glove box, then take out the gun Dada left for us.

It's heavy, heavy enough to remind me what it's capable of. Gah. I hate guns. The idea of doing to any human body what was done to mine revolts me to my core.

I hand it to Geraldo. He takes the weapon and flicks off the safety, leaving the cell phone in his lap.

I catch sight of the screen. It's frozen. The same red dot. The same mapped area where it started. My pulse spikes. Heat rises into my throat.

"She's here!" Geraldo had said, but Tony told me the phone would give me last known location, not her current address.

The screen is frozen. What was it Tony said about Jammers? They have a limited range? Dada disappeared to Tony's equipment when she went into the building, but I lost connection with her long before that. I lost connection with her the moment she put the bug on Armand.

I should've realized, but I'd been panicking. A cold spike of knowing works its way down my spine. How difficult would it have been for Geraldo to flick a switch in his pocket, turn on a device that blocked the signal? Not hard at all, not for him, who has all sorts of mechanical know-how.

I look up from the phone. Geraldo is staring at me. He cringes, nods his head. Pointing the gun at me, he says, "Sorry, mate," a perfect mimic of my accent. "Let's go find your whore."

Chapter 27

Dada

The basement has a low ceiling, dim lighting, and cinderblock walls. There's a blood-stained mattress in one corner and a rusted tank dripping oil in the other. There's nothing close enough for me to dart behind. The stairs are two steps behind me. There's no other exit.

Rosa is chained to a water pipe. Armand has his gun pointed at her head. I have my gun pointed at his chest.

Every breath I take is laced with the metallic odor of blood, dried oil, and dread. My chest has grown tight. My heart pounds in my ears. Sweat rolls down my face.

I say, knowing it for true, "If you shoot her, I will shoot you in the stomach then drag you to Walid's so he can finish the job. I'm sure he'll be displeased to know you're stealing his *merchandise.*"

For a moment, Armand's eyes go wide with surprise, then his lids lower and he laughs. "Who do you think he'd torture more? Me—someone who can make amends and offer him part of my success—or you—someone who is obviously *not* a nun and has aligned with Juan the Forger to try to get into Walid's confidence? Do you know he really likes his victims to be pretty? Like Juan."

He laughs.

The idea of Sean in Walid's hands sends a burst of rage through my body. I'm not Justice. I'm not a great shot, but I'm tempted to try for his skull. Could he pull the trigger on Rosa? If I shot him in the head, could he?

Ay. Dios. It's not something I'm willing to risk.

I need him to focus on me, need him to make a mistake that allows me to take the shot. "I'm leaving." I back up. "I don't want any part of this."

"Don't you fucking move!"

He turns his gun on me.

I shoot, hitting him in the chest. He falls back. I begin to move when there's a crashing sound on the stairs, then Rosa screams, "No!"

I start to turn, but something smashes into the side of my head. I slam to the floor, blinded by pain, gasping for air, and inhaling blood.

I cough, try to roll to my feet, but end up basically rocking. I've lost track of my gun. I've—

There's shouting and shots are fired.

Vision blurry, head aching, I crack open one eye and see Armand's dead body. To the left of him, struggling to reach Armand's gun, just out of her grasp, is Rosa.

There's scuffling in the basement and cursing. Blinking my one eye—I can't seem to open the right one—I gasp in confusion. Sean fights with… Geraldo?

Sean lands a blow that slams into Geraldo's cheekbone. Geraldo's head knocks back, blood spurting from the wound.

A smile cracks his face. He licks blood off his lips and tries to circle right. His eyes dart to the floor.

A gun? Did Sean knock it from his hand?

"Gotta go through me, mate," Sean says.

"No problemo, viejo," Geraldo says, in a voice as free from hesitation as it is clear. He throws a wild right jab.

Sean easily avoids it, then hits Geraldo with a fierce combination.

Geraldo staggers and slips, then dives for the gun.

He grabs it. Gun in hand, he rolls, aims.

I scream.

Sean grabs Geraldo's hands, lifts so the gun is facing the ceiling. They began fighting, wrestling over the gun.

They fall with the gun clutched between them. They're too close together for me to see what's happening.

I roll to my knees but tumble back down. Struggling, I drag myself back up and crawl, searching for my own weapon.

There.

I edge forward—my vision rocking like a boat on a turbulent sea—and grab it just as *bam, bam, bam* fills the room.

My ears ring as everything goes silent.

Sean.

He wouldn't shoot. He would be shot instead. With a cry that's part wounded animal and part avenging demon, I grab my gun and rock onto my feet.

The smell of gunpowder clings to the room. Sean and Geraldo are so still, a mass of unmoving bodies. There's a groan.

Not Sean. Sean hasn't moved.

Arms straining, head pounding, feet braced, I raise my weapon, hurt and terrified and ready to finish this madness.

Geraldo throws Sean off of him.

I moan out loud in pain and fury.

Wait. No.

Geraldo didn't throw Sean off. Sean rolled off. Pushing with his feet against Geraldo, Sean slides away, holding the weapon in both of his shaking hands.

Geraldo groans in pain, clutches a large, point-blank wound in his stomach. Blood pours from the wound. His face has gone white.

Sean gets to his feet.

I watch, unable to speak as he moves toward me, weapon down, hands bloody. I begin to tremble.

"Luv," he says, and I'm surprised by how calm his voice sounds. "I need to see if you're okay. Please. Put down the gun."

"What?"

"The gun, luv," he repeats.

Oh, I'm aiming my weapon at Geraldo, who's moaning and grasping at his stomach. There's no reason to point my weapon at a man who is helpless.

I lower my gun.

Sean is beside me immediately, putting a hand to my bleeding head. "Are you okay? What day is it?"

"I'm…" I blink my one eye and see the tears rolling down his face. "Mi amor," I say, realizing what he did, what he had to do, for *me*… because I dragged him into this. "Lo siento. I'm so sorry. I'm…"

"No." He shakes his head firmly. "No, luv. Fate offered me the choice. Life or death. Live with the woman I love or die with her. I chose. I chose for us."

He kisses me firmly on the mouth. Tears block my throat before they fall from my eyes. I want to say *I love you, too*. I want to say I'm sorry, but I can't force my voice through the lump of emotion blocking my throat.

"Ayudame," Rosa says, and her cry for help breaks us apart. Sean goes to her.

I move over to Geraldo. My knees land in his blood. "Let me see your wound."

"Stay away." His bloodied hands swing at me. After a lifetime of using anger and force, he expects them to simply keep working.

Not anymore. When he swung, I saw his wound. He's bleeding out. There's nothing that can be done.

Perhaps realizing this or seeing it in my eyes, he begs, "End me."

I have no intention of doing that for him. I will, however, give him something he has never given others. Hope. "Answer me and I will."

He nods and I ask, "You killed her. Your fiancée. Comandante Javier was right."

Again, he nods, seeking my eyes, seeking the person he thinks will end his pain. "Yes." He bites out the word through pain clenched teeth. "He wanted to arrest me."

Although there are still many details unanswered, some of it clicks into place for me. "You made a plan to throw Javier off the trail. You had Armand beat you up to make it look like you were attacked."

Geraldo looks down at his stomach, at all the blood, and says, "He enjoyed it, beating me. Nearly killed me."

"But it worked," I say. "You came out of it as a man who'd almost died looking for his fiancée. And, with a brain injury—a fake injury."

"You are both monsters," Rosa says, and I startle, realizing Sean has freed Rosa and both are right behind me.

"Mama." Geraldo begins to tremble. "So cold. Cold."

I grab for Sean's hand and he's there. I squeeze. "Not long now," I tell Geraldo. "Not long."

Geraldo closes his eyes. "Empty and cold," he whispers, and inhales deeply, so deep it rattles in his chest before he goes absolutely still.

Chapter 28

Dada

Back in my room at the convent, aching head propped on a pillow against my headboard, I try not to flinch at the glaring condemnation in my brother's eyes.

Hard not to do, since he's seated on a wooden chair by my bed, looking equal parts agitated and worried. If it was only anger, I might've had a shot. I look away.

"I'm pulling you," he says again.

"No." I look back and wag a finger at him, electing to not shake my head in emphasis because this concussion has made me so woozy. That's what happens when a two-hundred-pound man slams a gun into the side of your skull. Still, it was worth the wound. If Geraldo hadn't hit me, Sean never would've been able to knock the gun from his hand. "You're overreacting, hermano."

"The fuck I am. Your cover is blown."

"No, it's not. Sean never mentioned me to the policia. He told them that, after news broke about bodies being found in the desert; he'd become more vigilant He said he'd followed Geraldo because he'd been acting oddly—speaking full sentences when he was supposed to have a brain injury, making trips out at all hours. Now, the policia have their men, the records of the customers—thanks to Armand's meticulous notes—and the investigators are slowly identifying the women and notifying families."

Tony frowns. "What about Walid? He's got no idea who you are?"

"None. And now that Sean is working directly for Walid, we have more access to the traffickers than before. Getting information will be more straightforward. I'm established here. Visiting Sylvia, as the other sisters now do to pray with her and help heal her broken heart, means I can come and go from his building without suspicion."

"This isn't about where you landed. It's about where you've been. You got sloppy. You missed the guy."

Verdad. True enough. "How was I to know that Geraldo and Armand were brothers? They didn't look anything alike."

Tony holds his arm next to mine.

I harrumph. "Eso es diferente. We're adopted. And that wasn't the only way they were different. There was literally no way to tell—"

"Bullshit. You missed it. Geraldo set you up. He gave Sean the coordinates, right? That's what you said."

"Sí. But hindsight is twenty-twenty."

It all makes sense now that I know Armand and Geraldo's story. Armand had his real birth certificate in his home. His real name was Ramiro Chavez. Research enabled us to find information on his mother, also listed on the certificate. She was murdered. The word *whore* was carved over and over again on her body.

He might've seen the murder and been scared enough to want to align himself with the killer and not the killed, or maybe he committed the murder. Either way, after that death, the sixteen-year-old Armand carried his infant brother all the way here from Panama. The child had barely been alive when they'd gotten here. He'd anonymously given the boy to the sisters, knowing they'd take care of him, then had found a way to survive by working with the cartels in town. Until he'd met Walid.

The rest I've deduced myself. It seems Armand had been poisoning his brother's mind for years. In doing so, he made another like himself. And as Sylvia—God grant her peace—became older, Armand took a greater interest in rearing his brother. Two ruthless brothers not unlike Walid. Like draws like, Momma always says.

"Admit it," Tony says. He is very stubborn.

"Verdad. It appears Geraldo tried to kill Sean and me."

"Appears? Geraldo led you in there, then set off the explosion."

"Ah," I say, holding up a finger. "So I *didn't* miss any tripwire. That's one thing I did right."

"You took coordinates from the killer. A guy who, knowing where you'se were going, camped close by and waited."

"Sí. It was a mistake. But not enough reason to pull me."

Tony's eyes nearly pop from his head. I've seen him mad before, but not like this. This is a different kind of mad. This is a "you scared me senseless" kind of mad. That is why I'm managing to hold onto calm, even though he's being a pendejo.

Tony drags a hand down his face. "All it takes is one mistake, D. That's it. One. You and Justice are going to be the death of me."

That's highly offensive. Despite her skills with a gun, Justice is a hot head that refuses to listen to others. "I'm not like Justice."

Tony rolls his head around on his neck. "You're more like her than you think. If you weren't, you'd leave."

"I'm not done here."

"You are. Thanks to you, Momma and The Guild got Rosa and Carlos into Canada with their relatives. The legit way. Not Sean's way."

"Hey," I say, on the defensive, though I'm thrilled to hear Rosa and Carlos are doing well. She has a job at a daycare where Carlos goes. "He was doing the best he could for a woman he feared would be hurt in a very unfortunate situation."

Tony's eyelids lower with suspicion. "This is about him—your informant, Sean?"

"I don't know what you mean."

He snorts. "He was here when I got here, you know. While you were sleeping. I saw the way he looked at you."

I'm not going anywhere near that minefield. I purse my lips and ignore him—except, no one in my family takes well to being ignored and Tony isn't one for tiptoeing past a subject.

"You know, D, he looks at you like you're sleeping together and he'd give his right ball to see that keeps happening."

Rude. Also true. "That's none of your concern."

"You kiddin' me? Fuck. I'm pulling you."

"No. You aren't."

"The hell—

"You need me." My head starts to pound. I'm feeling nauseous, but I have to win this argument. I won't let him pull me. I won't leave Sean behind to finish this mission without me. "More importantly, you need Sean. We'll be able to get so much more information now that he's in-house. I believe we can close this whole thing out by the end of the year. Maybe sooner."

That stops him. He waits a beat. "That thing you said before, about Walid needing a new head of security. That true?"

"It is," I say. Now it's my turn to be wary. "You have someone you can sneak into the job?"

"I'm not sure." He looks away, rubs at the back of his neck. "What if it turns out I do? Would you be willing to swap you staying here for helping me get my guy in there and keeping quiet about it?"

This sounds unscrupulous. It also sounds like I'm staying in Mexico. Since I can't get Sean to abandon his search for Sofía—not that I'd ever ask—not to mention, his commitment to bring down the traffickers, I'm willing to do nearly anything to stay here with him until this is done. "Yes."

Tony stands abruptly, strides across my room and curses. "Fuck." He turns to me. "This is the last near-death experience you get. Next time, I pull you."

Smiling at the win, I hold out my arms to him. He grudgingly comes over, sits on the side of the bed, then hugs me tight. Too tight.

His voice breaks when he whispers in my ear, "Be careful, D. I can't lose you."

"You won't," I tell him. "No one is going to die on this mission."

"Oh yeah? We're that good?"

"We're that determined," I say. "*And* that good."

Chapter 29

Sean

Darkness soaks into my bones and sweet exhaustion weights my legs. I long for a few more moments of holding Dada, but it's too dangerous now that I've managed to get in with Walid.

She has to leave while it's still dark out. She begins to roll out of my arms.

I hold on, refusing to let go.

She kisses my lips. "I should go."

I run a finger down the smooth skin of her arm. "A minute, luv. A minute more." I pull her closer. "You in my arms… It's precious. Not to be rushed. One more breath, one more inhale of your sweet skin before you have to leave. That's what I need."

She relents and relaxes back into my arms, only to push back up when her cell phone rings. It's her official cell. The one I've come to dread hearing. She rolls over and picks it up from beside the bed. Much to my surprise, she presses the speaker phone.

Go," she says.

"Go where?" a male voice snaps.

"Tony, why are you calling?"

Sensing her unease, my heart begins to pound in my chest. I move closer to Dada and closer to the cell.

"Fuck. Am I on speakerphone?"

"Yes," Dada says, throttling the phone like it's a person. "Now out with it."

"Is *he* there?"

"Out with it."

Tony curses then exhales then says, “We found Sofía.”

I let out a whoop that’s part relief, part joy, and partly a way to keep myself from full out weeping. “Is she okay then?”

“I knew he was there.”

“Tony, mate, is she safe?”

“She’s safe, and not to be messed with. She helped us rescue her. Kind of a bad ass that kid.”

My throat fills with heat, as Dada wipes away a tear that’s tracing down my cheek. “Can I talk with her? Is she there?”

“Fuck, no. That’s not how this works, Sean. She’s got clearance to get through, doctors to see, and therapists.” He pauses a beat and adds, “I’ll let you know.”

That’ll do. “Thanks, mate,” I manage, choked up beyond words and beyond grateful that she’s safe and being cared for.

“Gracias, hermano,” Dada says, before wiping the last of my tears and kissing me gently on the lips.

“Thank me by doing your job and getting where you fucking need to be.” He hangs up.

Tossing her phone, Dada wraps her arms around me, kisses me again and again. Slowly, I begin to believe it’s all real. I kiss her back until I’m aching to be inside her.

Breathing heavily, I say, “I’m not sure one man deserves so much good fortune in one day,” I clear my throat and squeeze her close. “You’re here, luv. Sofía’s safe.”

“Better than safe. I intend to get all the details on how she helped those who went in to rescue her.”

I smile against her lips. “All this time, I’d imagined Sofía as the child who needed me and my help, but that clever lass showed me she was a survivor. I’m grateful to know it, and even more set on following her lead by taking down those who hurt her.”

“Which is why,” Dada kisses each of my checks before pushing gently away from me as I groan my despair. “I have to get,” she lowers her voice, “where I fucking need to be.”

We laugh. She yawns exaggeratedly as she climbs out of bed and says, “And me with barely two hours’ sleep.”

I grin, remembering how she coaxed me from sleep this morning. I'd woken, moaning and throbbing, to find she had my cock in her mouth. "Hottest thing I've ever awaken to."

She sighs and stares longingly at me. "One day, we'll be able to stay in bed together, Sean." She blows me a kiss.

Ach. She's so beautiful. "You've perfected walking away, luv."

She shakes her bottom at me.

"That's torture. Get back here."

Laughing evilly, she closes the bathroom door.

I relax back into the pillow and drift off, thinking of the best wake-up call of my life.

Then Dada screams.

I throw myself out of bed and charge into the bathroom.

She's perched on the edge of the tub…and points down.

What the bloody hell?

I burst into laughter. "Really, luv? It's a *spider*."

"A spider the size of my foot. I've incapacitated it. Take it outside."

Incapacitated? The spider—it *is* actually pretty damn big—doesn't move. Ach, she's hit it with my shaving gel. Not dead, but, as she said, woozy.

I bend toward it. "Up close it's definitely not average size."

She snorts. "You two should get along well, then."

"Flattery won't change the fact that you owe me for this." Opening the cabinet, I pull out a dustpan and slide it under the spider's heavy body.

I maneuver the monstrosity out of the bathroom, through the room, and onto the fire escape. I leave the dustpan, because… *ick*. I shut and lock the window. Can never be too certain.

Returning to the bathroom, I find my woman still holding the shower curtain rod.

Have to admit that's exactly where I'd wanted her.

I shut the door, then crook my finger at her. "Need some comforting?"

With as much moxie as I've come to expect from her, she climbs down from the tub, walks forward, and slams into me, fast and hard.

Which makes me hard. Fast.

I wrap my arms around her as she kisses my chest and rubs my cock with hands that shake. Nothing gets the motor going quicker than a near-death experience.

My body responds in a way that's all about keeping her safe and taking her, here and now. I grasp her fine butt with a grip that intends to do both.

Kissing her, I lift her onto the sink.

Her soft lips cling to mine. Her skim my chest. Her legs wrap around me so tightly, I'm at a loss when she grabs my cock and presses me to her opening.

She is so wet. Needing no more invite, I push in with a groan.

Feels incredible, being inside her without a condom. I thrust into her softness, and she moans and mewls, a soft, needful sound. She's doing me in with those sounds.

Near mindless for her, I pump inside her heat, taking her with every bit of need and want, the power of it speaking for my heart.

Whimpering and moaning, writhing and rocking, she cries out, then bites down on my shoulder as she comes hard. The tension of her teeth on my skin feels about as good as the hot sound of her moaning in ecstasy.

Mindless with desire, I keep thrusting madly, ignoring the *bang, bang, bang* of my knees against the cabinet doors, for the *yes, yes, yes* of my cock pushing inside her.

Energy and need coils in my balls, rides my skin, and overcomes my every sense. My hands clutch her ass hard as I groan out my release, toppling over the edge into pure bliss.

I moan into her ear, trembling with pleasure, pushing into all her wet warmth until I'm satiated and exhausted. I rest my check on the top her head. Her face is buried in my shoulder. "I love you."

She smiles against my neck and whispers, "I love you. *Querido, eres mi mundo.*"

"And you're my world." I, kiss her softly on the head. We're still for a moment before something occurs to me. "You're on the pill, luv, right?"

SPOILER ALERT. SPOILER ALERT. SPOILER ALERT.
SPOILER ALERT. SPOILER ALERT.

Dearest reader,

Be warned that the following link is to a BONUS CHAPTER that takes you three years into the future of the Parish family. It contains an entire series' worth of spoilers. Good and yummy spoilers abound! If you hate spoilers, you should wait to finish the series before embarking on this tell-a-tale epilogue. You have been warned! If you've read the series or don't care a bit about spoilers, click the link and enjoy the chapter.

Your faithful author,
Diana

BONUS CHAPTER LINK:

https://BookHip.com/XQKGGTB

Acknowledgments

I'd like to thank my editor, Mackenzie Walton, for her incredible talent and insights. She helped transform this manuscript, making it so much more than it would have been without her.

I'd like to thank Daniel Ladinsky for allowing me to use part of his translation of St. Catherine's poem from his marvelous book, *Love Poems From God: Twelve Sacred Voices from the East and West*.

A huge thank-you to my copy editor and production editor, Judi Fennell. I sincerely appreciate all of your hard work and advice as I've navigated this self-publishing process.

To my incredible cover designer, Elizabeth Mackey, I can't thank you enough for your incredible artistic talent. You managed to create a gorgeous cover that captured my story and my heart.

Another big and beautiful thank you goes to my Advanced Reader Team. You all provide me with valuable insight and support. I truly appreciate each and every one of you.

Finally, a heaping helping of my gratitude to all of you who have read this book and series. It's a pleasure for me to share this world and these people with all of you.

About the Author

Diana Muñoz Stewart is a bestselling author who writes romantic suspense with a focus on diverse characters, action, adventure, family, and love. Her work has been praised as high-octane, edgy, sexy, and fast-paced.

Diana's work has been a BookPage Top 15 Romance, a Night Owl Top Pick, an Amazon Book of the Month, an Amazon Editor's pick, a Pages From The Heart Winner, a Book Page Top Pick, Golden Heart® Finalist, Daphne du Maurier Finalist, A Gateway to the Best Winner, and has reached #1 category bestseller on Amazon multiple times.

Diana lives in an often chaotic and always welcoming home that—depending on the day—can hold husband, kids, extended family, friends, and a canine or two. A believer in the power of words to heal and connect, Diana has written multiple spotlight pieces on the strong, diverse women changing the world. Sign up for her newsletter to receive the latest information on her new releases: https://dianamunozstewart.com/newsletter/

www.ingramcontent.com/pod-product-compliance
Lightning Source LLC
Chambersburg PA
CBHW072240190626
46809CB00018B/2858
9781951467111